# One More Time

Cover Design:
Letitia Hasser, RBA Designs

Photo Credit:
Sara Eirew Photography

Interior Design & Formatting:
Christine Borgford, Type A Formatting

# ABOUT THIS BOOK

*Ten years ago we were the toast of the town.*

Tanner's acting career had just begun. He was hotter than the stage lights and twice as captivating. The gorgeous Australian A-lister was everyone's teenage dream. And he'd picked me. Or so I thought, until he proved to be as false as everything else about Hollywood.

Now I've finally scored the perfect opportunity to star in a major film. The kicker? Tanner will be my costar. I don't know if I can do this one more time....

*Right now we're the talk of the town.*

Jenna's even more beautiful than she was the last time we were together. And just like before, I can't keep my hands off her. She still doesn't know the truth. The secret of what really happened back then.

Now I have the length of this shoot to convince her to re-write our script. But if I have her one more time, will once ever be enough?

# One More Time

## LAURELIN PAIGE

# ONE

*Jenna*

**W**HY AM I DOING THIS *to myself?* I wonder, as I sneak a sip of co-conut water between reps of hundreds. *I could be sleeping instead of being tortured.*

Next to me, I hear a text followed by a squeal, and I remember exactly why I'm doing this to myself. Because—*that*. I want *that!*

To understand what it's like to be an actress in Los Angeles, there's no need to eavesdrop at the hottest talent agency in town. Don't bother snagging a table at the latest vegan Mexican-fusion restaurant. Skip the shopping session at Fred Segal, the highlight at Sally Hershberger, and all the star-studded movie premieres.

To get the real insight, just sign up for Jake Frente's Monday morning Hot Pilates class at Model Body Studios. In his class are forty girls glistening with the perfect amount of sweat while perched atop tribal printed yoga mats working out to the beats of whatever rapper everyone is obsessed with that month.

And every single one of them will have a cell phone neatly placed on the top right corner of her mat, screen up.

For reasons I can't pinpoint, this particular class is completely full of A-list actresses–the kind that can expect a call at any moment–even during her 8:00 a.m. Monday morning workout. And Model Body Studios is the kind of place that welcomes the distraction of a cell phone ring (or *three*) in the middle of the abs circuit. If phones are ringing during Jake's class that means he's teaching the right girls.

The right girls . . . And me.

I have been occupying the back left corner of Jake's 8:00 a.m. class for the past four years without a single phone ring. Somewhere around year two I *thought* my phone went off, but it was a storm warning. Sometime around year three I begged my best friend to call during the class, but he got the time wrong.

Any day now, Jake is going to realize that I'm the least successful person in this room, and ask me to leave. I've started bringing him cold-pressed green juices—his favorite—to hold off the inevitable for just that much longer. Surely, if I just get in enough time around these women, whatever combination of luck and fairy dust they have will settle on me, too.

The whole thing is even more annoyingly ironic because I am the only model among this sea of actresses at Model Body Studios. My agent Carrie says I need to stop calling myself a model and start exclusively saying *actress*. It would be easier to agree if my resume wasn't so heavily filled with runway and commercial spots.

Or if she'd called to say so during planks in Jake's class.

I was discovered at the Short Hills Mall on my twelfth birthday. For a little more irony, the scout noticed me because I was doing an impression of Julia Roberts in *Pretty Woman* for my best friend Cassie.

Acting has been my dream for as long as I can remember.

I told that to the scout that day at the mall, confused when he asked if I would ever consider a career in modeling. After all, I wasn't striking poses to attract his attention. I was re-enacting the "big mistake" moment from Rodeo Drive outside of Sweetsy's Candy. I'll never forget the words he said to me as he passed along his card.

"Baby, I'm going to make you a supermodel, and then every single movie studio will come calling."

And even though it gave me the squicks to hear him call me baby, he was right about the first part. By the time I was sixteen, I was all but living in first class, shuttling between magazine cover shoots in New York, runway gigs in Paris, and all the most fabulous designer parties in Milan.

It was a fantasy life. I felt like an overnight princess plucked from suburban New Jersey and placed in someone else's magical world. There were fifty-foot yachts and masquerade balls and insane gifts from top designers. Men swooned over my every move.

They didn't want to hear me speak, though. I didn't need skills, I just needed to maintain my waistline. And at sixteen, that didn't require hot Pilates. At sixteen, it didn't matter that much to me that I was only a pretty face.

And if the trade off was loneliness? Well, my bank account sure wasn't. And there were always new movies to watch. I memorized monologues with the gusto of any theater student, alone in the home theaters of Dolce and Gabbana, or Anna Wintour, while the rest of the fashion world partied above me.

Honestly, I could have gone on that way for ages, if it weren't for two things. The first was the fact that models have a shorter shelf life than the average NFL player. Five years is an eternity on the runway. When I started to get fewer calls from all the designers who'd called me their muse only last season, I knew it was time to start working toward my retirement.

Retirement. In my twenties.

My modeling agency fulfilled their promise of setting me up with a talent agency and letting me spend more time in LA. That was four years ago. Today my time is *still* spent shooting lingerie ads in cold photo studios and waiting for my phone to be the one that finally rings in Jake's class.

*Please, don't let me be a has-been at twenty-nine.*

"Ladies! Up for the standing abs sequence!" Jake bellows from his spot at the front of the room.

I both love and loathe this day. The start of the week means casting calls, aka hope. But it also means grinning and bearing it through another round of Model Body as everyone else gets the calls for parts I auditioned for.

"We all know it's three weeks 'til the start of awards season!" Jake adds with a wink, as he adds a little extra gusto to his twisties. I add some to mine, too. If I can't be his most successful student, I can damn well be his most vivacious one.

And then, as if on cue, we hear the first phone ring of class.

*Shoot me.*

This time the phone keeps ringing. *Unbelievable.*

I look around, hoping the scowl on my face doesn't appear as obvious as it feels. But as I do, I see thirty-nine faces scowling back at *me.* (Forty if you count Jake.)

And then it hits me—it's *my* phone.

My first instinct is to leap into the air like the final scene of The Breakfast Club, but all eyes are literally on me. I play it cool, making a faux-apologetic face as I grab my mat and bolt for the exit. Grinning at Jake as I walk out, I'm gratified to see him wink back. Looks like this might have bought me a little longer in his universe.

"Hello!" I say. If this is a sales call, I will track them down and murder them.

"Jenna Stahl? I have Carrie Bonnaview for you."

"Oh, my *agent?*" I say out loud. The receptionists sure don't look like they care, but I do. I care that *someone* in this building knows I'm worth a Monday-morning call. And the women who collect my registration fees are as good as any. "Sure. Put her through," I say.

I cradle my phone under my neck so my hands are free. My palms are sweaty and I rub them down my thighs. I've been reduced to a terrified newbie. This call means everything to me. Not only is my career hinging on a role, and soon, my savings account is too. I roll up my yoga mat in the lobby and leave the studio as if to say, *this call is so important that it will take up the entire rest of class.* Really, it's so no one hears my voice quaver, or sees how my hands shake as I wait to hear if I've just booked a commercial, or a pilot.

"Jenna? Hello, Jenna?" Carrie says as I walk toward my car.

I grab the phone again with my hand, nearly dropping it as I maneuver. "Yes! Hi! Omigod hi!"

"Let me guess," she says, "You're at Model Body?"

"It's Monday morning. Where else would I be?"

"Well your *omigod* is valid. I have huge news. You're being offered a part in a movie."

"Define *a part*. Not to be ungrateful, but we've been down this road before." Unfortunately, I know I have a tendency to be cast as the girl in the movie that seduces the male lead for one scene and then disappears, the main purpose of my character to give every male in the audience a hard-on. Nine times out of ten, this seduction happens while my character is wearing a very low-cut top, or a bikini.

"This is not a boob part, Jenna. This is a lead. *The* lead in an incredibly charming, brilliantly written rom-com called *Reason To Love*. And it gets better. It's a Polly Kemper film."

My heart jumps, once, before exploding into a million shards of so much excitement and gratitude. I can't believe I'm still holding the phone.

I *worship* Polly Kemper, and I am not alone. She is an inspiration and an icon. We're the same age, but instead of languishing in exercise class, she's been busy directing not one but *two* of the top-grossing romantic comedies of the past five years. She's known for writing strong but lovable women and—most importantly—she has a track record for breaking out new talent.

I feel something, and realize that I am doing a tiny jig in the parking lot. Anyone inside Model Body can see how dorky I'm being, but I don't even care. I have been offered a part in my dream movie. It is *finally* coming together. My patience is paying off. I'll be able to afford another four years in LA, even if I don't book a single other role.

"Yes, yes, yes!" I scream like that famous scene from *When Harry Met Sally*. "Tell them I'll do it!"

"Great . . ." There's hesitation in her voice.

"What?" I ask, my breath coming rapid and shallow.

"There's a catch."

"What? Low pay? Rough shooting schedule? Do I have to wear some metal bathing suit a la Princess Leia or something? Honestly Carrie, I don't care. I need this job."

"Your co-star is Tanner James," she says matter-of-factly.

My heart-sparkles dim, then go out. The pieces come back together and land directly in the bottom of my stomach with a miserable, painful *thud*.

Tanner James. Tanner *fucking* James.

The second reason my life changed, and the one I wish I could forget. Most days, I can. Most nights, I can't stop remembering. One thing's for sure—I'd rather give up my acting dreams forever than appear in a single scene with the man who broke my heart.

Broke *me*.

Of all the actors in the entire world, why did it have to be him?

"Jenna? Hello? Are you listening to me?" Carrie says. "I know this is hard to hear, but they want you *because* of the idea of you and Tanner. A *Janner* reunion will play huge at the box office, especially since it's been ten years since you broke up. You two have high nostalgia value. You're Justin and Britney. Ben and Jen—No! Jen and *Brad*. Just suffer through this and Hollywood will kneel at your feet, I promise . . . Jenna? Are you still there?"

"Yeah," I say, blinking back tears. I don't think I've ever suffered a bigger disappointment. Well—just that once. And he's the reason this is ruined, too. "I'm here. Tell Polly Kemper that I'm very sorry, but I can't accept the role."

"Wait! Please don't make a decision now. Let's talk this out. Come over to my office and we'll pow-wow. I'll have my assistant order food. Or drinks. Or a therapist. Anything you need, honey."

The lump in my throat makes it hard to talk, so I keep it simple. "I'm sorry."

I don't even wait for a response. I hang up the phone, get in my car, and hope this was all just a bad dream. That any second now, the blare of my alarm will wake me up, and I'll have to get ready for Model Body.

Ten minutes later I'm still sitting in the studio's parking lot, and I no longer think that there's any hope at all that this isn't real. I need to get out of here before class gets out, but my brain is doing too many backflips to even think about starting the car, let alone driving.

I know, objectively, that Carrie is right. The world lost its mind when Tanner and I broke up. I can only imagine how nuts they'd go for an on-screen reunion. We'd all make more money than we could spend in a lifetime.

But those people weren't living my life as they gossiped about me from behind their screens. They have no idea how painful it was to *live* through that. To them, I'm not a real person. No one here in La La Land is. We exist for their attention alone.

Ironically, at one time I did only exist for attention alone. For *Tanner's* attention. Because I confused it for love.

The sudden surge of anger I feel at that empty thought finally propels me to turn the keys in the ignition, and head home where I spend the rest of my day rage-cleaning and reading scripts for other, less high-profile jobs, trying to block out the memory of today's glorious and terrible offer.

Finally, after hours of distracting myself, I decide that what I really need is a nice, long bath.

I pour my favorite lavender salts into the water. I hesitate only for a second before I grab a sleeve of Thin Mints, rationalizing that I did *some* Pilates, after all. I turn on Adele and slip off the athletic pants and tank I've been wearing since I left Jake's class, then slide down into the warm bubbles. I make a mental note to send him something nice, seeing as I didn't just take my call outside, but ditched him entirely. He doesn't need to know the role was a bust.

God, he *can't* know. I'd be mortified.

I need something to take my mind off the situation. Some online shopping in my happy place should do the trick. I grab my cell phone and hop on ShopChic.com. I scroll through the sale section, hoping for some trendy yet neutral tops I can wear to auditions. All I see, though, are party dresses. The kind that in another life, I might wear to my Polly Kemper movie wrap party.

Even the thought of her name is enough pressure on the floodgates to let all my earlier angst to come rushing back in. I don't know what's more upsetting—that my dream was so close to being within reach or that Tanner is in my head again.

So much for relaxing.

Why would he even consider agreeing to star opposite me?

Because it's a good publicity stunt. That's why.

I hold my breath and slip beneath the surface, as though I can drown away this truth.

The only reason the man who shattered my entire world would agree to do a feature movie with me is that he cares about publicity more than about what we once had. And I'm the only one who still thinks about our past. He never cared at all. The memory of our relationship means nothing but dollars in his bank account.

My stomach twists at the thought.

I knew he was a heartbreaker, but could he actually be completely heartless? Tanner James was my everything. My first LA kiss, my first love, the man I gave my virginity to.

The thought of that night slips into my mind. I picture the off-the-shoulder red dress I wore to channel Julia Roberts for the night. Everyone says your first time is awkward and fumbling and painful. But mine? It was bliss. The thought of it makes the space between my thighs light up. I can feel the tingling pull, begging me to touch, pleading for release. But there's no way I'm letting Tanner James get the best of my fantasies right now.

He's done it too many times already.

That thought shifts me from nostalgic to furious. In the ten years since our breakup, I still haven't discovered any other ways to think about him. Longing and anger are all I have. I flip from the ShopChic page I've been mindlessly staring at to a new window—TMI, the biggest source for celebrity gossip. I need to know if there's anything else that could be behind this decision of Tanner's. A scandal he's trying to hide. Or maybe his last movie didn't do as well at the box office as projected, and he needs the money. Anything would be better than believing he simply has no respect for what we once were.

I start to type Tanner's name into the TMI search field, but as I do something else catches my eye. A headline.

*Gem Charles—the new body of Marissa's Closet.*

My heart lands in my stomach for the second time in under twelve hours. Marissa's Closet is my biggest account.

Or . . . it was.

I click through to the article, which starts with five full-screen shots of Gem in the latest style of lingerie I've been promoting for the past eleven years. *Marissa turns heads with a fresh new British face*, the caption reads.

"We've been so lucky to work with the best and most beautiful models," says CEO Marissa Sutherland, "Our brand has always been about what's new and next, and we think Gem Charles is the epitome of fresh."

She may as well have said, "Jenna Stahl is staler than old bread."

I shouldn't be crushed. I know exactly how this business works. I was once the sixteen-year old that pushed all the other "supers" off the covers of the glossies. I know about the limited shelf life of a career in this industry. I *know*. So why do I have this sick feeling over it?

I guess there's a difference in knowing "the end is near," versus learning "the end already happened and no one bothered to tell you." I just thought I had more time.

A little bit more, anyway.

Acting has been my passion for so long, though I'm well aware it's not the typical path for ex-models. Some launch cosmetics lines. Others get involved in fashion design or become judges on reality shows. A few shift to being magazine columnists. The majority scout and coach fresh new faces. Only a few lucky ones make the move into acting. The ones who transition earlier have the best chance.

I regret the jobs I turned down when I was younger now the way I regret eating before a bikini shoot. When I was with Tanner, I had frequent opportunities I didn't take advantage of for one reason or another. I suppose I took it for granted that those parts would come just as easily later on.

Now, thanks to TMI, it seems the whole world knows I'm up the second-career creek without a paddle.

Without acting, I have no fallback. I have a GED, earned backstage at international Fashion Weeks, but no college education. I have no contacts anywhere but within my agency, and the various casting directors who have promised to keep my headshot on file. I know full well that file is a black hole. And no way am I moving back to Jersey.

Without acting, my future is a blank space.

And I don't just mean because I have no other job prospects. I have no other *life* prospects. I don't have a boyfriend-who-could-turn-husband-one-day. I don't have a volunteer-gig-that-could-turn-into-a-passion-project. I don't have a pet. I don't even have a plant. There's a great big hole of uncertainty waiting for me in the not-so-distant future and that void does nothing to heal the still-gaping hole inside me from the past.

I'm alone and lonely, and I can't even say I sacrificed love for an amazing career, because my career at the moment is a resume of boob parts and used-to-be-spokeswoman roles. No one would sacrifice shit for that resume.

I'm over and done.

But I don't have to be . . .

My mood has gone from "relax and forget" to "screw this and everyone" so fast it has whiplash.

I step out of the bathtub and slip into my robe without even wiping the lavender-scented bubbles off my soaking wet body. I stomp into the kitchen, open the freezer and grab the ice-cold bottle of vodka I keep on reserve for moments just like this one. I close my eyes and take a giant swig.

That one's for bravery. Once I'm sure it'll stay down, I take another, this one to numb the pain of what I'm about to do. Then I dial Carrie Bonnaview's cell.

"Please tell me you've come to your senses," she says without so much as a hello.

"I want to be very clear that this is going to be a strictly professional situation," I say. "I will go to work. I will *act* as Tanner's love interest. I will go home. No rumor mills buzzing about our reunion. No happy, lovey press shoots. This will be a j-o-b job."

"Is that a yes?"

"Yes?" I say. Then I say it again without the question in my tone.

"Yes. It's a yes."

I hear Carrie jumping up and down in her living room. I roll my eyes, but I know she's right to be excited. I should be, too. This is the break we've been waiting for years to materialize. This will be the thing to change my life. So why does my stomach suddenly feel like it's tied up in knots?

I bite my lip hard to keep the tears from welling up again as Carrie rattles off congratulations and a list of what happens next. I know I've made the right decision. It's the *only* decision if I want my future to be better than what currently seems possible.

I just wish a better future didn't depend so completely on the man who destroyed me in the past.

# TWO

---

*Tanner*

"ALL RIGHT, TANNER. WE'RE GOING to need a few more minutes to re-light before we get the last take here. You can hold out another fifteen minutes before lunch, right?"

If I had a dime for every time I got asked that question, I could open my own movie studio. It's not even a question, really. It's framed like a question to make me feel like I have a choice in the matter. To put me at ease. Really, it's a not so subtle reminder that if I fuck off to my trailer, people will remember.

*Hurry up and wait.*

Ask anyone in the film biz and they'll tell you, that's the phrase that defines set life, if not an actor's *entire* life. I spend more time waiting around than I do on camera. What do I really get paid millions of dollars for? Sitting patiently.

It's day one, shot one, and we've spent the past thirty-five minutes trying to decide if my character should arrive at this fake post office with the sun at his face or his back. The lighting guys are consulting with the camera operators who are talking to the director. It's a first day conversation. Everyone wants everything just right. There's a nervous energy on set. People are tiptoeing around me, making sure I'm as happy as possible at every single moment.

Except, of course, with no option of being happy in my trailer.

I get it. Doesn't mean I have to like it. But I put up with it because, even after more than sixteen years in the business, I'm still as in love with this insane industry as I was as a wide-eyed fifteen-year old full of fake confidence on the set of my very first movie back home in Sydney. Oh man, did I prep for that role. I was Teen Football Player Number Two. I had seven lines across two scenes. I spent all summer lifting in the gym and running dialogue with an acting coach to prepare.

I smile to myself thinking about how I've been working out and meeting with a coach the past few months in prep for *this* movie, too. Of course, I get paid a lot more to do it these days, an amount that a fifteen-year old me wouldn't have been able to fathom. But money is not my incentive for wanting to be perfect for this role.

"Okay, we're ready. We're going to roll it one more time," my director Polly calls out from her spot in Video Village.

Polly is one of the good ones, and I'm lucky to have her running the show. She started directing almost as young as I started acting, working her way up from short films shot in her parents' Ohio backyard to a booming career making tent-pole romantic comedies for all the major studios. I respect her hard work, and I appreciate her go-with-the-flow attitude.

She also couldn't care less about the fact that I'm famous. She's made no secret of the fact that she's here to build up women, not men. She doesn't put up with my shit. She doesn't kiss my ass.

I'll admit my ego doesn't always love these facts, but she keeps me on my toes, and my name wouldn't be on the project as a silent producer if I didn't think she was the right choice.

"Are you cool if I riff on the line a little?" I facetiously ask Polly as she settles into her director chair.

"Perhaps . . . but the line is *'thank you.'* Where exactly are you thinking of taking it?"

"I've been workshopping a few options. *Thanks. TY. Danke. Spank you.*"

Polly laughs. So far everything I've heard about working with her has been true. She's honest, she's to the point and she's all about doing whatever it takes to make her actors comfortable.

She's also well aware that the two actors she's working with on this particular project may need a little time to get comfortable—although she's not very likely to worry about *my* comfort as much as my co-star's.

Anyone who knows our history would feel the same.

I had a weird pang of nervousness when the call sheet got e-mailed out last night. Smack dab on the top under REASON TO LOVE was a name I never expected to see beside mine on this kind of document: It didn't feel real until I saw it in black and white, although in some ways, nothing had ever been more real.

Once upon a time, Jenna was *my* reason to love.

How quickly that once upon a time ended.

I immediately scrolled down the call sheet to see if we would be shooting together today, and I'd be lying if I said that I wasn't just a little disappointed to see that we were not. In fact, I haven't even bumped into her on set yet.

But that's about to change.

This morning we're shooting the post office scene that only features my character, Bobby. This afternoon they're shooting her at her character Grace's house. But from the looks of the schedule our paths will cross right around lunchtime at the craft services tent.

It's time for an "accidental" meeting.

Yes, I'm that mature. But, to be fair, I kind of feel like she's put me in this position.

Six months ago, when Jenna signed on to this project, I'd proposed the idea of us getting together for a coffee or something—anything—to talk over our past or the movie or just to break the ice. Whatever she wanted.

My agent talked to her agent talked to Jenna talked to my agent talked to me. It's like that Taylor Swift song, complete with informing me that Jenna had no interest. Zip. Nada. Not even in discussing the movie.

It's been ten years—you'd think hearing that she doesn't want to see me would have stopped hurting by now. But Jenna's a wound that won't heal.

Maybe all first loves are. Still, I have a feeling Jenna's especially hard to get over.

I blame that on her too. She hates confrontation so much, she acts like she's allergic to it. For as long as I knew her, she would tie herself into the most complicated knots to avoid it. I'm sure it's why she never wanted to meet face to face before the shoot, but it's also why I haven't had closure after all these years. I'd thought when she agreed to the movie deal that it must mean that she was finally ready to talk. Ready to listen.

But maybe it just means she's moved on.

Well, good for her. She's lucky she could. That makes one of us at least.

And she—or maybe *her* agent—made the choice to keep us apart until we absolutely had to meet. Was that smart? I don't know. Perhaps. The last thing either of us needs is to mess up Polly's movie with our personal baggage. What if we'd met and fought? Or worse, met and realized we no longer have an ounce of chemistry, and we were still obliged to fake it for the screen?

But our personal baggage is what the world wants to see. It's the story they're paying for, not the one we're filming.

And I can't imagine a world where Tanner James and Jenna Stahl don't create fireworks on sight.

And those extra months without meeting *did* give me the chance to hit the gym. I've gone from muscular to ripped in some kind of attempt to either impress her, or hide my nervousness under layers of biceps. I guess in some ways I'm still that same fifteen-year old over-prepping for the role. Only on this set, I'm also playing a second role: Jenna Stahl's ex.

It's the one I've been playing for ten years. It's the hardest role I've ever played, a role I never deserved to play, though try telling that to anyone else. No one blames her for casting me in it.

I've run this interaction over and over again in my mind, perhaps more than my actual lines. I've decided I'm going to play it calm and cool, but genuine. As though it's only been a short time since I've seen her, as though so much between us hasn't remained unsaid. I can't scare her off now that I'm this close.

First, I need to pull her aside, into a quiet corner. This requires no audience, not even a single girl from Makeup eavesdropping while looking for the vinaigrette. First, I'll compliment her about something to break the tension.

That shouldn't be hard. Jenna has always been the most beautiful girl on earth.

With any luck, that will disarm her, lead her into a conversation. I have this dumb idea that if I can just be *near* her long enough, I can remind her of how things were. How *we* were. Before everything.

*Hey Jenna. Nice to see you. Your hair looks great like that.*

She'll politely repay the nicety—Jenna is nothing if not polite—and then right after that I'm going to launch into my proposition. This situation is awkward, but I'm excited about seeing her again. I'll say something like, *Let's have dinner. I think it could help us get our footing, especially with our characters. There are some things we never got to talk through.*

Just thinking about seeing her makes me so nervous my palms start to sweat. It's a wonder I can concentrate on my lines.

"Alright. I think we've got it!" Polly yells out. "Congrats on not messing up your very first scene, Sir James."

"Oh shit," I call back, "Was I supposed to be wearing pants this whole time?"

"Very funny."

And there's my first scene, officially wrapped. But the real work is still ahead of me.

I don't even change out of wardrobe before starting the walk over from the post office set to where craft services is set up around the corner. I want to make sure I get to Jenna before everyone starts lining up for food. But then I see all the groups of people gathering and chatting, and I realize my whole plan is about to be a bust.

There *is* no quiet space to say hello. Cameramen are yelling to grips that are throwing foil-wrapped tacos over the heads of production assistants. It's a rowdy first-day food fest, and now I have to pull off an awkward interaction in plain view of a hundred people who are fully aware of my past—*our* past. I need a plan B, quick.

Or a miracle.

I'm standing just outside the large tent where food is served, trying to come up with a fast fix when I see someone turn the corner from where the trailers are parked and throw a beaming smile right in my direction. It honestly takes me a second to recognize her. I knew she was a knockout. I've followed her modeling career. Watched her grow up in front of the camera.

Just—I didn't expect her to look so *happy*.

I look behind me, there must be someone else she's throwing these sunbeams at, but no. It's me. And all the warmth of a summer day surrounds me at the sight of her walking toward me. Her dark hair is long, spilling past her shoulders in waves. Her creamy skin is translucent, her blue eyes bright. My cock jumps in my pants as she brushes a curl back, exposing that swan-like neck I used to love kissing.

She's got a look in her eyes that I swear I've seen before—the night I met her.

I was at a JD Hawkins party at the old Spanish mansion he was renting off Mulholland. The pool was jam packed with famous faces and new stars. I was a nineteen-year-old hotshot, not looking for anything but a good time. If the chick in the pink bikini gave me the eye again, I was going to offer her one too.

But when I locked eyes with Jenna across the pool, all that went out the window. She looked at me with an intensity that no one ever has again. It's the same intensity I see in her eyes this very moment.

*Shit.*

All of my anxiety about this hello might be for nothing. Am I really the only one of us who is carrying any baggage from our past?

"Tanner," Jenna says as she finally reaches me. "Nice to see you."

"Yeah. Wow. Hi. How are—?" I'm caught off guard, but I know my lines.

Before I can get to them, though, she takes over.

"I'm great. Listen. We're both adults, and I'm looking forward to getting this job done as professionally as possible. We'll stick to the script.

We'll interact when we have to. I'll respect your personal space, and I'm hoping you're capable of the same. What's done is done, and I frankly have no interest in rehashing any of it for the benefit of other people. So I'd rather not exchange numbers or spend time reminiscing about the past. We're here to do a job. And that's that. Are we good? Good." Her lips find their way into another radiant smile.

I'm still trying to process the speech she just delivered when she holds out her hand. In fact, I'm so thrown that I don't even realize that she's reaching out for a handshake. A *handshake!* Like we're some kind of former business partners that had a deal go wrong. Like she didn't spend three years waking up naked in my bed. Like we didn't have a freaking celebrity gossip pet name.

I hated that dumb name, but right now what I hate more is the fact that the J-A part of it doesn't seem to remember that it ever existed. I want to remind her, I want to tell her that I'm *not* okay with this, that I'm anything but good, but—

Once again, Jenna walks away from me, trailing orange blossom scent behind her.

I don't know how long I stand here, staring after her, before a PA holding a taco comes by and asks if I'm okay.

"Fuck!" I yell. Immediately, I feel bad for startling him; his food is on the ground and he's unable to make eye contact. I want to say, *No dude, I am not okay. I just met a total stranger that I used to know as well as my own heart.* I want to say, *I haven't been okay in ten years. I just want a chance to say I'm sorry, but the person that I need to apologize to won't stop and listen.*

I run a hand through my hair and try to gather my shit.

"Look, bloke, I'm sorry," I say to the poor PA who's still standing there, his mouth open wide as he stares at me. "I'm hangry. I took it out on you. I'd love a taco." I don't fucking want a taco. But he seems happy to be able to help, and at least he's not staring at me anymore.

I take a deep breath in and then let it out slowly.

It takes a lot to shock me, but Jenna just accomplished the task. I can't remember ever seeing her so certain and strong. And it honestly didn't even sound like she rehearsed that little speech. She just waltzed right up to me and let it all go. Apparently a person *can* fundamentally change. I don't know whether Jenna Stahl went to a therapist or a witch doctor, but someone turned her into a completely different person.

Maybe it's a sign that everything I did back then—or didn't do, rather—was the right thing after all.

Unfortunately for me, the only thing changed is her personality. Because the rest of her is even more drop-dead gorgeous than she was the day I met her at that pool. And I'm ready to follow her into the deep end all over again.

Or maybe I already have, because I feel like I'm drowning now that she's soaked all my plans.

"Here, man," the PA says, reappearing with a taco and a bottled water. "Break a leg for the rest of day one!"

*Day one. How many days does that leave me to find the girl I knew in the woman I see now?*

There are a dozen people in front of her in line, and at least the same amount behind, plus a sea of people casually eating lunch and chatting all around. But all my eyes will focus on is Jenna.

All this time worrying about how she'll fit in here, and instead I'm the one who's the dickhead.

But then again, where Jenna is concerned, maybe I always was.

# THREE

---

*Jenna*

GRAB MY LUNCH TO go and run back to my trailer, slam the door behind me, and actually breathe for the first time since my moment with Tanner. My mind is racing. My body is shaking. I want to jump up and down and scream. I want to re-live every second of it over and over again. But I also wish I'd never done it at all.

Honestly, I have no idea how I feel.

I'm a mess.

On one hand, I have never felt so powerful—so *badass*. On the other, confrontation has always left me quivering and anxious, my stomach in knots and my thoughts tangled up—and that's when it *doesn't* involve Tanner James.

Thank God Walter made me practice my speech a thousand times, practice it until I knew it backwards, practice it until I didn't have to think about the words that poured out of my mouth as naturally as though I'd only just that moment thought them.

Because being that close to him again, smelling his cologne?

It made me remember all the good things about him, too.

I just cannot believe I actually pulled it off.

I shoot Walter a thumbs-up selfie text, complete with a praise hands emoji, so he knows I didn't choke. Even though when I saw Tanner's sculpted face, that artfully tousled hair, I almost did. Almost fled to my trailer to cry. Almost leapt into his arms and started stripping.

Ten years, and I still want to kill him and fuck him all at once.

I grab a Pellegrino that I *so* wish was something stronger from the trailer fridge and sit down on the couch to try and relax. Get my head clear before I go do my job. After all, that's why I'm here, I remind myself. Not because of *him*. Because of work. I only have fifteen minutes before they're scheduled to call me for my very first scene of my very first day of my very first leading film role.

I could scream with excitement over that, but I know that I'm already dangerously close to losing my cool. I'd always thought by the time I broke into acting, I'd be confident and cool, but every corner I turn makes me feel like a giddy teenager. A terrified, giddy teenager.

My emotions are all over the place. I grab my script and try to focus on my lines.

Of course, I have no luck. My mind is trapped in a loop, reliving the scene between us over and over. Did Tanner notice that it was totally rehearsed? Could he see the pounding of my heart through my chest? Did he notice how I swayed when he spoke—his Australian accent making me weak in the knees like it always had? Was that weird look on his face shock or anger . . . or delight?

And why can't I remember what happened in that moment when I'm having zero trouble remembering what he looked like from top to bottom as I approached him on the lot?

I knew it was a mistake to let my eyes explore him as I walked up to say my piece, but they were drawn to him like a magnet. His tight T-shirt revealed some pretty serious pecs underneath, much bigger than I remember.

Tanner always worked out like a fiend before starting on a new film project. I remember loving those times when we were together. He would wake up before the crack of dawn, run to the gym for a session and then come home to me sweaty and full of energy. Did he still spend his mornings that same way? And if so, who did he come home to now?

My excitement settles thinking of Tanner with other women. It's been ten years—how many have there been?

I've tried not to read about him, and I've done a pretty good job of avoiding most gossip about him, even though I've watched every one of his films. Several times, if I'm honest. Now I'm overcome with a powerful need to know *every* detail of his life, compare it to the one I once shared with him. To trace his path away from me, pinpoint what his new women have that I hadn't. Or was I just the first in a trail of broken hearts?

I pick up my phone to start a search but stop myself when his face comes back into my mind, unbidden, the slow confused blink he gave before accepting my handshake.

His T-shirt wasn't quite long enough to tuck into his crisp, dark jeans so I caught a glimpse of the white ridge of his boxer briefs sticking out from the top of his waistline. Calvin Kleins, as always. Tanner had done a Calvin ad back when we were dating and they'd given him a lifetime supply of underwear in gratitude. He used to wear them around the condo with absolutely nothing else on top or bottom while doing his impression of Mark Wahlberg, the original king of the Calvins. I'd always catch him flexing in the kitchen while doing the world's worst Boston accent.

The sight of that thin cotton stretched against his tight ass and large bulge is seared in my brain, so much so that it was one of the first images that popped up as I walked over to him today, ten years later. I wonder if he feels as good as I remember . . .

*Focus, Jenna! And not on that.*

Doing a Google search on his life isn't going to be helpful either. I trade my phone for my script.

But I know these lines, I've been running them with Walter for six months and my mind goes back to marveling at the fact that I pulled off my speech without melting into a giant puddle. It was a win, and a first in many ways. I don't do conflict. I never have.

One time I'd mustered enough courage to tell off a mean-girl model who'd been treating Hair and Makeup like her personal servants backstage at a Roberto Cavalli show, but then I stuttered my speech to her like a two-year old and ran away in tears while every single model in the show stood staring. And that was basically the one time I ever tried. It's not only that I hate confrontation, I'm just plain bad at it.

That speech to Tanner? It was not only my first successful confrontation, but it will likely be my last. I got it all out, and I'm proud of myself. But now I'm done.

*You know playing it safe is the fastest way to the middle, Jenna.*

I hear those words in my head as if Tanner was whispering them in my ear right here in the trailer. It makes the hair on my neck stand up. Tanner always wanted to push me outside my comfort zone. He believed I could handle anything, even my greatest fears. When we were together, I believed him, too.

*"I can't read your mind, Jenna,"* he'd say. *"You have to tell me how you feel, even if you're afraid it's going to make me mad. You're safe with me. We'll figure it out."*

He made me feel like I could take risks because he would be there to pick me up if I fell. And he always was—right up until he wasn't.

My thoughts wander back to the past, to days I haven't let myself think about in a long time. I was seventeen and a virgin when we met. He was two years older and experienced. We had the spotlight in common—how many people could possibly know the loneliness of being a teenager in the public eye all day only to come home at night to an empty hotel room? His family was half a world away. My mother was too busy raising my three siblings. Our friends from before we'd become famous didn't understand. We'd gotten each other when no one else did.

That summer, I was riding the high of my first *Vogue* cover, wearing a million-dollar dress I'd inspired my favorite designer to make. I was on my way to being a star. But Tanner? He was a comet, blazing fire. At first I was self-conscious, worried that my inexperience would turn him off, but it only seemed to intrigue him more.

I was the luckiest girl in California.

I was the luckiest girl in the world.

And one morning I woke up and realized I was in love. Funny how the biggest mistakes come wrapped in the most beautiful packaging.

That night, he'd been honored with a huge award by the Producer's Guild—*Best New Acting Talent*. The critics had raved about his performance in *The Jet*, calling it a shockingly human portrayal of the superhero no one thought had a heart. He'd single-handedly taken Jet from obscure comic about a frankly problematic character to the hottest new franchise onscreen.

And he was being recognized for that. It was the award that all Tanner's idols had won, and he was over the moon. All his dreams were coming true, and I wanted to give him a gift of my own. After the ceremony, we attended the official after-party at the Infinity Lounge at Hotel Nitro on Sunset—the hottest spot to open that summer. It was on the thirty-fifth floor of the building, so high that you could see straight from the beaches of Malibu to the fully lit Hollywood sign. All the hottest actors, producers and directors were swarming around him with congrats and promises of even bigger projects, but his eyes were only on me.

I'd worn red, and he'd told me I was devastating in it.

"Five more minutes and then we're running away," he'd breathed in my ear, the warmth sending delicious shivers down my spine. I felt drunk on him, on the realization of the depth of my feelings, on the secret I was keeping—that tonight was the night. I only wanted to be with him, beneath him, in a gorgeous hotel room below all the party madness. I kissed him and told him I'd be waiting in our bed.

*Our bed*, he'd mouthed back, as it dawned on him what I was saying. He pulled me close and kissed me again, deeply, a promise of what was soon to follow, in front of everyone. Agents, producers, press, they all watched as he took my hand in his and together we ran, me in heels, gasping with laughter as he pulled me along and out of the party.

We didn't head down to a hotel room, though. He took me back to his apartment. He said that he wanted me to be comfortable in his bed, *our bed*, he'd repeated my words, for my first time. His sweetness gave me the courage I needed to stand before him and offer myself.

The weight of his gaze as it swept up and down my body felt more valuable than the luxurious red silk puddled at my feet. I stepped out of it, still in my heels, toward him. In that moment, I was fearless. He held out his hand for me again, and together we walked toward his bedroom, him removing and then tossing his tie onto the sectional as we passed.

Once inside the cool confines of his room, Tanner pressed me up against his bedroom door. His breath was on my neck, then my lips, then at my ear, tracing a path I longed for him to follow with his mouth. Goosebumps sprang up all over my skin in response.

"Yes?" he asked.

"God, yes," I said without a second thought. My legs quivered in anticipation of his next move. I wanted him to rip my lingerie off and place his cool hands on my now searing skin.

But he didn't. He moved slowly. He brought his lips to my cheek and kissed me so softly that all I could feel was his breath. I shivered as a jolt pulsed through my body, right down to my core. His mouth moved from my cheek down to my chin.

*Another jolt.*

Then he dragged his mouth ever so gently from my chin down my neck, mapping every inch as though it was precious real estate. I could feel myself growing wet, and I marveled that only a few such feather-light touches could have such an effect on me.

Moving along, he landed kisses on my collarbone, his tongue dancing along my clavicle, then tracing a path to my breasts. I hissed and threw my head back, not wanting anything to obstruct his path.

"Perfect girl," he murmured. "So greedy for this. I'm going to ruin you for anyone else."

My breath came rapidly, and my head was already spinning as I whispered back, "There will never be anyone else."

I had been worried that I wouldn't know what to do—too inexperienced to meet his deft moves with my own—but in that moment instinct took over, I drew his mouth to my own, tugging at his bottom lip and teasing him until he grabbed my thighs and hoisted them to his own, lifting me into the air. I folded my legs around him, wrapped my arms tight around his neck, and we made promises with our kisses as he walked us to the bed.

He laid me down gently among the pillows, and I watched hungrily as he slowly unbuttoned his shirt to expose the superhero-perfect chest half of America was dreaming about. Wanting to match him move for move, to offer not only my innocence, but my willingness, I pushed myself up and removed my bra.

My breasts, more than a few runway casting directors had told me, were too full for my body, and I'd always been vaguely annoyed by that. Now, seeing the look of wonder on Tanner's face as they spilled out for him, I suddenly saw them in a different light. Maybe they weren't made for a runway. Maybe they'd been made for *him* all along.

He bent over me and drew one finger down the slope of my breast, watching my face carefully as he stilled at the very tip of my peaked nipple. I could feel my eyes and mouth growing wide, could feel that they were no longer controlled by me, but by the pleasure he gave me. Tanner must have seen it too, because he gave a wicked smile and pinched my nipple.

The noise that came out of my mouth was somewhere in between a gasp and a scream, and it only made him smile all the wider at me.

"So responsive," he said. "Can you feel your pussy answering me, too?"

I gasped again, at the word he'd used. In my world, *pussy* was a commodity, something the rich men at the fancy parties thought you owed them when they granted you the favor of allowing you on their arms.

I didn't know it could sound so . . . *sensual.*

I tried it out. "My pussy . . . my pussy is so wet right now, Tanner. I want you."

It had to have been the clumsiest attempt at dirty talk he'd ever heard, but it made him groan as his hand strayed toward the bulge in his pants.

In that moment, I felt so powerful that I could cause this kind of reaction in The Jet.

In no time at all, he'd undone his pants and flattened his hands under his boxer-briefs to slide everything down his legs at the same time. Even as he bent over to remove them, I was straining to see that part of him he'd freed, to find things to say about it that would please him the way my last try had.

"Let me see your cock," I commanded, my voice still containing the tiniest quiver that betrayed me. But Tanner stood up straight, taking me seriously, letting me take all the time I wanted to gaze at the way his hardness jutted proudly from his flat abs.

I wasn't completely unfamiliar with his body, but the fumbling hand jobs I'd given him during hot make out sessions were a far cry from being allowed to peruse his body like the work of art it truly was. He'd sculpted every inch of it himself with hours at the gym. And the pinnacle of everything, there, standing stiff and tall, perfectly pink and ridged was answering me the same way my pussy did for him.

"Do you want to touch?" he asked.

I nodded, biting my kiss-swollen lip and reaching out.

"Not me. *You.*"

I stared at him, ascertaining if he was serious, and his darkened eyes stared back. Perfectly serious, and perfectly lustful. I may have been a virgin, but I was no stranger to my own touch. This was a pose I had perfected, a show I knew just how to put on.

I mirrored his actions in sliding my hands under the sides of my lace panties, red to match my dress, of course, and bent my knees up to pull them off.

I lay there before him, completely naked, entirely exposed, wearing nothing but the sky-high strappy heels I'd worn beneath my gown. My eyes scanned his as I tried to decide how I felt. In fashion, model bodies are treated exactly the same way that mannequin bodies are. I'd been nude in front of hundreds of other models as we hastily changed backstage while the crew milled around us. More times than I could ever count, designers had watched me put on their clothing with nothing between me and it to create unnecessary lines.

None of that had ever made me feel vulnerable. If anything, it had made it easy to see my body as utilitarian, a thing that belonged to me and happened to be both useful and valuable.

What I decided, as my fingers stole down my waxed mound to the edge of my wetness, was that this didn't make me feel vulnerable either. It made me feel at home in my skin in a whole new way. Now my body was a thing that belonged to him, too, and happened to be made for pleasure.

And when my fingers dipped and circled, as I parted my lips with my other hand, I showed him exactly how to give me that pleasure.

He watched me as I watched him. His eyes were on my hands demonstrating the places that I'd discovered made my toes curl, and mine were on his long, hard body as he crawled onto the bed and between my legs. When his face was right there, I let my hands fall away and almost screamed again at the sensation when he replaced them with his warm, wet tongue.

And, oh, how he'd paid attention to my lesson, as he first drew the flat of his tongue up my seam slowly before flicking the sensitive bundle of nerves he found with the tip of it.

When I'd circled my finger slowly around my entrance, he'd noticed and did the same with his mouth. The swirling of his tongue matched the feeling in my head that was somehow also building up from the tips of my toes. Before I even had a chance to say a word, I was spinning wildly through space, barely registering that his first two fingers had slipped inside me just at my point of climax, giving my inner walls something to grip as they convulsed in ecstasy.

The satisfaction I felt as I slowly fell back to earth was short-lived, because Tanner was already kissing his way up to my breasts. The soft skin bruised before my eyes as he nibbled softly, reigniting the fire in my core.

He drew first one nipple into his mouth, then the other, as my hips bucked against him, desperate for more.

As delicious as it felt, what he was doing, I needed a more active role. I needed his mouth on mine. I needed to wordlessly say what I didn't have the vocabulary to tell him. My hands tangled in his hair, pulled his head up to mine, and he knew what I wanted. His arm snaked out to open the bedside drawer, to pull out the condom I was both glad he had and regretful to use.

With a final kiss, Tanner pushed up and away from me, so that we could both look down as he first rolled the latex down his shaft, and then lined up at my entrance. The pressure at my hole alarmed and aroused me at once, which he instinctively seemed to realize. He shifted his weight to his left arm so that his right hand could come play.

Only seconds later, my body was humming again, my legs falling farther apart as he strummed me with his fingers and pressed against the gentle resistance with his cock, until finally, with a cry, I allowed him entrance. He froze, inside me, fingers still applying just the tiniest amount of pressure, playing my body like an instrument.

We stayed there like that, looking down at the place we had become one and then back into each other's eyes, for an eternity, for a second, for as long as it took our heartbeats to synchronize.

When I was ready, I relaxed my upper body as my hips shifted slightly up. Slowly, slowly, he eased both all the way in and all the way down, so that we could kiss again as our bodies learned each other's most intimate secrets. Gradually, he pushed and pulled, each motion tinged with the edge of pain, which gave way bit by bit to pleasure.

We rocked together, each other's anchors, in the sea together now, until we spiraled into a hurricane as one, coming and coming and gasping our love into each other's mouths.

After, we lay cuddled and entangled, as close as two people can be outside the act itself, and told other secrets. Tanner always worried he wasn't a good actor and couldn't believe anyone had taken a chance on him. With his gorgeous face and body, he'd frequently been steered toward modeling growing up in Australia, but he hadn't been willing to settle. He'd wanted to engage creatively. He'd been passionate about wanting to make characters come to life. Standing and posing wasn't going to cut it.

Hearing that gave me the confidence to tell him that I wanted the same. I held my breath, expecting Tanner to laugh or tell me I could probably get some parts based on my looks.

But he didn't do either.

"Perfect girl," he'd whispered, punctuating it with a kiss, *"you'll* be the only one who will ever hold you back."

At the time, I had closed my eyes and lost myself in his ministrations, but his words have returned to me a thousand times since.

Had he known me that well? Or was he just familiar with the same self-doubt? Or had the moment our bodies joined for the first time carried so much power that the words he'd spoken had life? A prophecy made real by emotion.

The last thing I remember thinking that night was how secure I felt in his arms. The knowledge that I was loved, and cherished, even worshiped. It gave me a sense of home I'd not had in three trips around the globe.

But all of that's a memory now. One I'd be better off forgetting. Just because Tanner encouraged me to get where I am today doesn't mean anything. Just because I once called him home doesn't mean there's any place for me in his life anymore.

I'll respect his personal space. We're adults. We're professionals. We're good.

I seem to have convinced Tanner. If I say it enough times, maybe I'll believe it, too.

# FOUR

*Tanner*

I N SOME PARTS OF THE world, rain on an important day is considered bad luck. Since we're in Los Angeles, where drought is part of everyday life, the mood is a combination of cheer and wariness. Every time thunder booms and lightning brightens the sky, everyone on set jumps. We need the moisture, but we aren't used to the accompanying show.

It's three hours into what is scheduled to be a twelve-hour day and we're already two scenes behind. It's raining hard enough that the camera operators have to cover their gear and their bodies in special tech ponchos, but I'm still holding out hope that the clouds will close so we can finally get to the scene we've been delaying for the past hour.

Right now I'm starting to think I'm not going to get my way.

Hurry up and wait. Again.

I usually handle the on set stop and go with a good amount of patience. Today, not so much. It's taking all the energy in my body not to bite every nail off my fingers. People are huddled in the craft services tent, sipping steaming cups of coffee and chatting while I just want to scream at them to move the entire set to a soundstage so we can get moving already.

Today has to go perfectly.

It's the day that Jenna and I are shooting our first scene together. Or, it's *supposed* to be the day. For the past sixty minutes we've been standing three feet from each other, not speaking, as the powers that be—in this case both Mother Nature and our director—decide our fate. Time spent not shooting costs money. I know this is as annoying to Polly as it is to me, if not more so, but I'm absorbed in my anxiety and can't believe that anyone is as worked up about this delay as I am.

As producers call studios, who call execs and watch the weather reports, Jenna whispers into her phone. Yeah, I'm watching her. I pretend to play Backgammon on mine, while sneaking sidelong glances and wondering if it's her new boyfriend she's whispering to. Wondering, if so, what he's like. Does he know about us? About our past? He must. Everyone does. I wonder if he's as jealous of me as I suddenly am of him.

Finally, she hangs up. And now we're just standing here, ignoring each other and waiting.

I take a deep breath and turn to talk to her, but think better of it. If she were interested in conversation, she'd at least have looked at me. My breath whooshes out, enough to cause her to glance my way. When our eyes meet, I feel a jolt of electricity and I could swear I see some softness there before the disinterest slides in.

She's quick to look back down at her phone, but I stare just a little longer. Long enough to fix her in my head to enjoy later—probably while jerking off in my trailer.

That should take the edge off.

The Kelly green sundress she's wearing is cut short, allowing those famous mile-long legs to take center stage. As I gaze at her, a gust of wind billows through, lifting her dress just enough for me to see a peek of the lacy panties beneath, just enough to tease me. She still likes to match her underwear to her outfit, I see. I look forward again just before she catches me looking, and I see her smoothing the fabric back down out of the corner of my eye.

It takes every skill I've ever learned to keep my pants from tenting like a primary school boy in front of the cheer squad. *Do not think about*

*Jenna in a cheer uniform*, I scold myself, and it's only the next crash of thunder that knocks the idea out of my mind just in time. When Jenna startles at it, I actually take a step in her direction, the action so natural that it takes a second before I remember that she doesn't want me to hold her. That I'm not her comfort anymore.

It's fucking torture.

Being in such close proximity to her has my head messed up, and the past bleeds into the present. Was it really all that long ago that we were so easy together? We would have huddled to watch this storm in each other's arms, maybe snuck off to fool around behind the fake post office while everyone was busy deciding what to do next.

"Everyone listen up!" Polly yells as she jogs over. "We're postponing this for weather, moving onto the next scene. You know what to do!"

There is an audible groan across the lawn where a couple dozen people have spent several long hours setting a picnic scene, and then shielding it from the rain. If I'm frustrated with the pace today, I can't imagine how the crew feels.

I turn to Jenna, hoping for the chance to turn this into a conversation, but the set of her shoulders tells me she's upset. My mouth opens again to break our silence, then, almost as if she anticipates it, her jaw tightens. It hits me that maybe she isn't ready for the next scene. It wasn't on the schedule, and she's new to all this. She might not know that on set, you have to be ready for anything.

If her lines are what's bothering her, that won't matter. The PA will feed them to her if need be, and we have time to rehearse a bit while the next set is prepared.

I should tell her that.

Okay, it's just an excuse to talk to her, but I'm desperate to break the silence. But just as I turn to her and open my mouth to speak, Polly finishes her instructions to her assistant director and turns to us.

"Jenna, Tanner, can I talk to you about something for a second?" she asks. She looks almost as tense as Jenna does. What the hell is going on?

Then it hits me.

If we're skipping scenes twenty-four and twenty-seven because we can't shoot outdoors, that means we're jumping to scene eighteen—the next number on the call sheet.

Oh, shit. Scene eighteen.

Films always shoot out of order. There are a number of reasons—daylight, weather, locations, availability—that mean the production schedule is carefully designed to be as efficient as possible, divas not-withstanding. What it means for the actors is that the very first scene we perform can end up being the movie's climax, or a huge emotional moment, or a silly comedy bit inside a dramatic film.

Or, in this case, it can mean that the first time I face Jenna on set, it will also be the first time we kiss on-screen.

"So," Polly says as she pulls us both off to the side, "Are you guys ready for this? Jenna?"

I watch some of the tension drain out of her posture as she smiles at our director.

"Totally fine." And weirdly, she now looks like she actually *is* fine. My mind returns to the one-sided conversation Jenna and I had yesterday. New Jenna isn't flustered by a thing. New Jenna is solid as a rock. New Jenna is *totally fine.*

So what was with the stiffness of a moment ago?

I have a sinking feeling that the real problem is me.

And once again, I'm the one standing here wondering if I only imag-ined how much we meant to each other back then, or if Jenna is simply better at moving on, getting over me as easily as last season's fashions.

"Tanner?" Polly asks, and I don't think it's the first time she's said it. I shake my head to regain my focus, and put on a smile of my own, the wide, reassuring one that's graced a hundred magazine covers. What kind of actor would I be if I couldn't pretend everything was fine while my heart cracks a little more under the weight of regret?

"Yeah. Of course," I say.

"Great. Let's run through the scene a few times so we can get you comfortable with the blocking and make sure you two are feeling nice and comfy. I'll get the DP so we can roll tape on it just in case."

"Perfect," I say, but as I do, Jenna also responds.

"That won't be necessary," she says. "I don't need to rehearse. Just show me where my marks are. I'm ready to get this wrapped. It's too chilly to stay in this dress much longer."

Not a single goosebump mars that perfectly creamy skin. She just wants to get *me* over with.

I'm desperate to get some kind of real emotion from her. Something that says kissing me for the first time in a decade means something. Anything. I'm a dick for needing to see it, but I do, and so I guess that's who I am.

"I don't know that a rush job is going to be good for the shot, Jenna," I pretend concern for the film. "It's the first kiss, after all. If we don't sell people on our relationship now, they aren't going to follow for the rest of the movie."

Polly's looking back and forth between us, as though she's willing to hear us both out.

"I think it would be wise to practice, even just one," I continue. "In my experience, a run-through really helps calm the nerves."

That was exactly the wrong thing to say, and I know it the second it's out of my mouth, but I'm too proud to apologize.

"I appreciate your advice," Jenna says back bitingly, "but I'm not nervous. And I'll assume with all *your experience* that neither are you. Now, if you'll excuse me, I need to get my makeup freshened before we call action." She stalks off, ass swishing invitingly as she does.

I watch her leave with a mixture of regret and arousal that Polly notices immediately.

"Seriously?" she says with chiding annoyance.

And I guess I've just alienated both the women I need to keep happy if we expect to pull this shoot off without any drama. I try the smile again, but Polly sees through me. In her mind, I've just proven myself to be exactly the kind of man she works hard to keep out of her movies.

Well. I was looking for her to show some real emotion. Guess I got it.

"Let's just go," I respond roughly, feeling worse than I have in recent memory, and knowing I can't take that into the shoot.

I spend the rest of my time before the clapper slams shut rolling my head from side to side and stretching, but nothing's going to get this knot out of my stomach.

The motions of the scene are simple. Jenna's character Grace walks into the restaurant lobby just as my character Bobby is walking out. She's looking for me, and I'm leaving to find her. We stop as we see each other. We both smile. Then there are four lines of dialogue before I cut her off and grab her for the kiss. It's quick and simple.

Or at least it ought to be.

But before Jenna even has her first line out, Polly leans forward and calls, "Cut." She walks over to have a quiet word. "Jenna, you seem . . . annoyed. Take a deep breath. Let go of any personal or real life emotions. Okay?" She breathes in and out with her star a few times, then nods for the second take to be called as she walks back behind the camera. "Action!"

This time Jenna gets the line out, but I'm the one who looks tense.

The third time, Jenna doesn't look at me.

The fourth, I'm talking too loudly.

Well, of course I am. We're three feet apart, the only two people in this fake lobby, we're talking to each other, and yet she still doesn't seem to *see* me at all.

"Cut!" Polly calls again, clearly exasperated. "You know what? I tried to do it your way, but this is a waste of everyone's time. We're all going to take five, and you two are going to talk this out."

Jenna crosses her arms and hangs her head as she blows out a long sigh through pursed lips. She seems embarrassed, and I get it. I feel chastised too.

Polly's right.

It's one thing for a director to use multiple takes to get the best possible performance, but we haven't even made it through those damn four lines. It isn't fair to her, it isn't fair to the crew, and it isn't fair to us. This is Jenna's big break, and rumors are going to start that she can't act, which couldn't be further from the truth. I started this bullshit earlier, and I'm the one who needs to end it.

"Look. I was an asshole," I say. She doesn't look up at me, but her arms uncross.

"You were."

"I wasn't—" My voice lowers, in both volume and pitch. "I didn't mean it like it came out. I just keep remembering my first day on set in a lead role and how uptight and nervous I was. Any second, I kept expecting someone to tell me I didn't belong there. I threw up twice between takes. I guess I was just thinking maybe you felt the same."

She doesn't say anything for a long moment. It stretches between us like taffy.

"I guess I understand that," she finally says. When she looks up, when her eyes meet mine, it's then I see something real behind her mask of indifference. I see the hurt and confusion and anger of three thousand six hundred fifty days in those bottomless pools of blue.

She doesn't let it stay for long.

With a blink, the mask slips back into place, but I'm strangely comforted. I may have ruined everything back then, but I didn't imagine that I meant something to her. It's not much, and it doesn't change anything now, yet it does all the same.

"Anyway, maybe it isn't a bad thing to be visibly nervous right now," she says. "First kisses are nerve wracking."

"Do you remember our first kiss?" It's out of my mouth before I can stop myself. I'm insane. We haven't had a conversation about normal stuff, and I'm already bringing up the past. I'm a total asshole.

I start to apologize again, to tell her never mind, but I hesitate when I glance over at her. She's looking away from me again, but her lips quirk up, and I know she's thinking about it. Thinking about our first kiss.

And now I'm thinking about it, too. It's as vivid to me as the green of her dress.

That night at the party on Mulholland, after our eyes met, after I'd recognized that single-minded intensity on the face of the most beautiful creature I'd ever laid eyes on, I'd started toward her. I had to know her name. Had to be near her.

I walked around the pool, around bodies and drinks and people trying to get my attention. It was all on her, and my eyes never wavered once from their target. She watched me the entire way. Her friends chattered around her, and she ignored them. Finally, I reached her. She pulled her lusciously full lower lip into her mouth, and bit gently. I could smell her perfume, something that reminded me of Southern California sunshine encompassed in a flower. Orange blossom, that's what it was. I opened my mouth, and—

"I dove backward into the pool," Jenna giggles at the memory. "I just knew you were going to use some terrible pickup line, and I couldn't bear it."

"I was just going to tell you my name," I protest indignantly, and not for the first time.

"I knew your name. Everyone did. And I wanted you to be as perfect as you looked in the picture I'd clipped from Hollywood Hotties and glued in my journal. And I knew you were going to ruin it by speaking. But there you were in the pool with me when I came up for air, opening your mouth again. So I—"

"Kissed me." I pressed my lips together, recalling the soft, yielding pressure of hers on mine, tangy with chlorine and sugary lip gloss. "You were so sure of yourself. So confident. This perfect girl. I was blown away."

"My heart was pounding out of my chest. I was kissing my movie-star crush. Everything else disappeared."

We aren't touching, but in this moment, we are completely together.

"Break's over, come on, we're burning—well, twilight!" Polly yells, and the spell is broken. Everyone scrambles back onto the set, noise flooding back in. We take our places again, and this time, I feel like myself, the self that has complete mastery over his career, if not his personal life.

"Camera speeding," the DP says.

"Quiet on the set." Polly commands. "Aanndd action."

Jenna rushes into the frame as I'm rushing out. We stop, just past each other, and angle back to stare at each other for a beat. We hit our marks, and it's just the right amount of time. The hum in the air says we all feel it, the actor's sixth sense that the scene is working.

"You're leaving," Jenna says. There's the right amount of excitement in her voice as she blurts her line as though it's completely spontaneous. Her eyes scan my face as though looking for answers.

"To find you," I reply, even though her character already knows.

"Well . . . here I am," she says. She adds a little catch in her voice after the *well* that I wasn't expecting. It makes her sound like she wasn't sure she would come. It makes her sound vulnerable, which is a smart acting choice. Then she reaches out and runs her finger along my shirt collar. "Look at you."

In that moment I don't feel like Bobby. I feel like myself.

And I feel like Jenna is seeing me as herself, not as Grace.

Even if that isn't true, and I'm projecting, I can tell it's exactly the right way to play this scene. The words may have been scripted in an over-air-conditioned room somewhere in Burbank, but the feelings behind them, the actions, are purely our own.

"Why would anyone look at *me* with you in the room?" I reply, and then without a thought as to where to place my hands on her face, or how quickly to make the move, I pull her in. My eyes search hers for a moment of doubt and don't find it. Once I'm certain, I tilt her chin up to me and as my lips land on hers, I come home.

I forget about the movie, though in my mind, we're whirling as though we're in one. Her mouth parts for me, but only the barest amount, and my tongue finds the softest match in hers, tasting of sparkling water and that honeyed flavor I always associate with Jenna.

No one is watching. Everyone is watching. It doesn't matter anymore.

Jenna and I have kissed all the ways, in all the places, and we've been damn good at it every single time. This one is no different. I stroke my thumb over her cheek, and her mouth opens even more, our tongues tangling as her breasts press against my body. Her familiar orange-blossom scent invades my nostrils. I've waited so long for this, but it's even better than I'd anticipated, and I press just a little more into her, to satisfy the growing hardness in my jeans . . .

"Go ahead and cut," Polly says.

. . . And with that I remember where I am. If I were the blushing sort, I'd be red right now.

"So much better. I honestly think we've got it, but let's do some more to catch some other angles."

I'm silent, and staring at my co-star, waiting for a sign, but Jenna has reverted back to professional actress mode. She's pulled out her phone, and is texting after a quick nod to Polly.

Was she really just *acting* the entire time? She's good. Better than I knew she'd be. I'm ready to award her an Oscar.

Me, on the other hand . . . I don't know what I am right now. But whatever it is, I have to rewind, recall my feelings, and experience this all over again so the cameras can get another shot.

We run the scene from the top. Jenna nails every moment, possibly even better this time. I touch her face just as perfectly and meet her lips just as naturally this second time and it transports me all over.

I wonder if the whole set can feel the connection we have, the chemistry that sparks and smokes and explodes like a mad scientist's kit every time we touch.

"Cut!" Polly yells again. "Wrapped. Nice work, everyone. See you bright and early, and hopefully in the sunlight." She hops down from her canvas chair to converse with the cinematographer.

Meanwhile, I turn to Jenna, ready to talk this out. But all the sweetness is gone from her face again.

"Thanks for the pep talk. See ya tomorrow," she says, already texting furiously as she starts to walk away. My entire life is starting to feel like a montage of scenes where I look after her as she walks away.

*I'm so stupid.*

Even if she can recall the feelings from the past for inspiration in a kissing scene, she'll also remember the other feelings. By reminding her of the good, I automatically remind her of the bad.

And besides—she's an actress. Better than I am. She's always been. I'm an idiot for believing the scene meant things would be different between us.

I change clothes at Wardrobe and start toward my trailer to collect tomorrow's call sheet and lines to take home. After briefly considering grabbing some beer on my way, I decide that won't do a thing but fuzz the edges of my already tenuous control.

I have to talk to Jenna.

It's the only way I'll get the answers I need to sleep tonight.

I walk up to her trailer door, but it's shut. I stand outside trying to decide if knocking is rude or fine, or if she's even there at all. But before I can make a decision, I hear her voice through the window. She's talking to someone, maybe on the phone? I can't make out any silhouettes through the curtains, and I definitely don't want to get any closer in case she can see out.

"I'm going to get through this, Walter," I hear her say. "But doing this movie might just be the worst mistake I've ever made."

Then she pauses, I assume to hear whatever *Walter* is saying back. The worst mistake she's ever made? That hits me hard in the gut. Am I really making her that miserable?

I'm so overwhelmed, I barely register the next thing she says.

"I know," Jenna coos, "I love you too. Bye."

Before, he was a hypothetical. Now I have a name for the bastard. A stupid name, too. *Walter.* She loves a guy named Walter.

I clench and unclench my fists. I automatically hate him.

Except, that's not true. It's me that I hate. I hate myself for trying to make peace with Jenna. I hate myself for caring about who she's dating.

But most of all, I hate myself for ever letting her go in the first place.

# FIVE

*Jenna*

THERE ARE TIMES WHEN YOU are kissing someone else, pressing your lips against them, and hoping they respond in kind. There are times when someone is kissing you, they're in charge, and you are passively receptive.

And then there are those magical moments when two people are kissing each other. Where you explore and claim, act and react, sharing your breath in perfect rhythm.

That is what it was like kissing Tanner today. How had I forgotten about that? About how even a simple kiss, the most basic expression of affection between two people, could feel more intimate than sex?

I remember now that it had always been like that with us. His mouth had always known just what to do against mine, and vice versa.

The barest brush of his lips had always left me hungry for more.

That would be acceptable, barely, on its own. I could come back here to my trailer, pull up my dress, and satisfy the aching want by myself. I could pretend that it was just the physical perfection of today's scene that had me in a tizzy.

But it isn't just the memory of his body weight settling between my legs that's been stirred up. It's my longing for the things that went along with perfect kisses. It's the hand holding, the late-night phone calls that went on until night disappeared into morning or we fell asleep with phones pressed between cheek and pillow.

It's the overwhelming urge I have to skip the rest of my solo scenes today and run to Tanner's trailer.

It's the realization that I'm not over him, and never will be.

I need to talk to someone, and it sure as hell isn't going to be Tanner. So far, I've hidden the pain this entire venture has caused me, and I'll be damned if I'm going to expose it now. Why would you offer a weapon to the person who used it on you before?

There's only one person in my life that I trust to honestly and compassionately give me some advice. I reach for my phone and hit my number one speed dial.

"Girl," comes the answer after only two rings, "what happened?"

Walter Harris—fashion designer and best friend extraordinaire—reading my mind before I even say a word.

Walter and I met almost ten years ago, when I judged a fashion design reality show for a season. He didn't win, but it was the producers, not the judges, who made that decision. I felt so bad, I hired him on the spot to design a gown for the Met Gala. All of three minutes into draping, we were giggling together so hard I ruined the pattern.

I've been the face and body of every W. Harris line ever since, and Walter has been my bestie and personal designer. It kills me that the world hasn't gone as gaga for his designs as they should, but I know Walter is one Vogue review away from fame, and I am doing everything in my power to make it happen, including a contractual obligation to use one of his looks for a huge scene in this movie.

Carrie thought I should have asked for more money, but I put my foot down. If I only get one diva moment in film, it's going to be beneficial for someone other than me.

"We did a kissing scene today," is all I have to say, and he groans as loudly as the springs on the bed I can hear him flopping down on. We've had a lot of gossip sessions snuggled up in his bed, eating popcorn and bitching about fashion.

One of the first things we bonded over, though, was heartbreak. Right around the same time Tanner was publicly humiliating me, a man named Roger was doing the same to Walter. Roger was his boss, to make matters even worse, and so Walter not only lost his relationship, he lost his job. Hence ending up on a reality show, instead of in an atelier like he should have.

Every single Fashion Week, tons of events and parties involve Walter and Roger pointedly ignoring each other, at least until the champagne starts flowing along with the insults. I once heard that following them is Anna Wintour's favorite pastime.

He's always been envious of my ability to avoid Tanner, and so he was completely horrified that I was voluntarily doing this movie. After reading me the riot act, though, he'd hardly stopped for a breath before plunking a mug of tea in my hand and starting work on my first-day speech.

Granted, he warned me it would take more than one speech to survive this shoot, but I'd also thought it would take more than one kiss to destroy me.

"How bad is it? If I had to kiss Roger in front of cameras, they'd probably also get a porn and then a snuff film out of it."

"Who would be doing the snuffing?" I ask before I can stop myself. "Never mind. Don't answer that. Suffice it to say, that's about the same predicament I'm in."

"Jenna, my love. There are going to be mixed emotions and confusing signs and a few quivers in your . . . lady parts during this shoot. The most important thing for you to remember is that this is a job, and you are a professional. It's just like that speech we wrote for you to slay Tanner with on day one. That is your first focus."

"Right. Yes. I am a pro. This is a job."

"Good. Say it every morning and every night. And remember, if you can get through this, you never have to see him again. At least, not after the press junket and all the premieres, that is." I can hear the teakettle whistling on his end, and a wave of homesickness washes over me. What I wouldn't give for a long, lavender-scented bath and a cup of Earl Grey.

Instead, I have two more scenes to pull myself together for and nail.

Movies, it turns out, are more exhausting than a full day of go-sees in Milan.

"This is not comforting," I tell him. "But I'm not going to break now."

"Damn right you're not! Jenna Stahl is a beast. Everyone knows it. You're the hardest-working girl in fashion; you aren't going to let a man fuck up your acting career. Let this fuel your fire, love."

"I am. I'm going to get through this, Walter. But doing this movie might just be the worst mistake of my life."

"That's your fear talking," Walter said in his sweetest big brother voice. "And you know you're stronger than all that. I love you, boo."

What would I do without my Walter?

"I know," I reply, "I love you too. Bye."

The minute I get off the phone with Walter, I feel relieved. He's right. I built my first career on long hours and by never allowing any frustration to show. I can do that here, too. Every bit of the confusion and angst I'm feeling can be channeled into my performance. I text my PA to grab some Earl Grey and meet me in Makeup to run lines.

I don't have a single Tanner scene for the rest of the week, and I am not going to spend that time dwelling. I'm going to spend it slaying.

——————◆——————

ONE WEEK AFTER *KISSGATE*, I'M proud to say that I have survived sans Walter. Mostly.

I did call him once when I was sure Tanner saw me completely naked while I changed from one costume to the next behind the wardrober's makeshift curtain, but it turned out to be a false alarm.

I survived the rest of the week with little to no Tanner interaction. That's because I'd been working on scenes with Kate, the actress that plays Grace's best friend Kit, and he'd been doing the same with his on-screen buddy Shawn. We were shooting just a few stages away from each other tons of times all week, but I engaged in some expert avoidance tactics to give myself a little space. Tactic one: eat lunch in my trailer. Who needs to get into the mess of people at the craft services tent when you can bring your own healthy food from home and enjoy it in the comfort of your "office?" Same goes for breaks. Yes, it is nice to chat with the crew, but not if there's a risk that someone with whom you do *not* want to chat joins the convo.

Do these moves sound somewhat juvenile? Perhaps. I don't love conflict, as has been pointed out to me by every family member, friend, and boyfriend . . . forever. But right now I have a very legitimate reason. I am at work, and I cannot blow this once-in-a-lifetime opportunity because of a boy. If that means a few solo lunches, so be it. I am a professional.

That is the mantra I repeat in my head as I walk from the safety of my trailer clear across the studio lot for the next scene of the day. Again, I'm shooting sans Tanner, so there should be nothing to worry about.

Then I see Angela Clark rushing toward me, arms flailing.

"Hi! This is perfect! I was just coming to get you! Somebody said you eat lunch alone in your trailer every day? What's that about?"

Angela is the publicist for this movie. She works for IK PR, one of the biggest firms in town. I know them well because they sent assistants swarming to every single restaurant, coffee shop, yoga class, and drug store run of mine after Tanner and I broke up. They were trying to sign me. They wanted to help, "guide me through this challenging time in the spotlight," they claimed. I successfully avoided them and any bad press back then, and yet here we are again.

What an annoying coincidence.

"We need to talk press," Angela says. The tone in her voice makes it sound like *press* is brain surgery.

"Sure," I say, "What's up?"

"No. We need to talk press with you and Tanner together."

"Why is that exactly?"

"Because you are co-stars in what is going to be the biggest romantic comedy since Meg Ryan and Tom Hanks were on screen. It is huge, and I need a strategy, especially considering your whole—"

"Fine," I say. I don't want to hear whatever it is Angela has to say about our whole anything.

"Let's arrange a lunch somewhere fab!"

By *somewhere fab* she means *somewhere public*. I've been around long enough to know the tricks of the PR trade. Angela takes Tanner and me somewhere for a bite then pops out to the bathroom leaving us alone at the very moment a paparazzo just so happens to walk by the table and snap a shot of us canoodling over sushi. *Boom!* We're all over the gossip magazines under headlines like, *Janner, Together Again?! Janner Swooning Over Sushi! Janner On AND Off Set Love??* It's the oldest trick in the book.

"Sorry, but I'm too busy to go off set. Let's just sit down and chat at the tables in the craft service tent tomorrow," I say and watch Angela's face fall.

My face, however, is beaming. I have somehow mustered the courage to stand up to this slippery pro, and I am incredibly proud. I cannot wait to tell Walter! He loves to say that there's a special place in hell for PR execs.

"*Boorriinngg,*" Angela says, "But fine. Do you want to tell Tanner?"

"No," I say, "you can tell him." And with that, I've successfully handled two conflicts in one conversation. My work here is done.

The next day I find Tanner and Angela at a table in the far corner of the food tent. It's a little more secluded than I would like, but there are still dozens of people swarming around. There's no way someone could sneak a picture without it being clear we're just on set, and that is not enough of a story for the gossip queens to promote. Of course we're on set together. They need more. Mission accomplished.

"Okay," Angela starts. "This might be a little awkward, but it's time for the firm to develop a strategic plan for feeding information about you two to the media and paparazzi."

"You need a strategy to leak stuff?" Tanner asks, as though he doesn't understand what she's talking about.

I let a smile sneak out. He sees and gives me a *these people* eye roll. I look away. We are not going to leave this meeting buddy-buddy.

"Yes, Tanner. The press is ravenous to find out more about a former celebrity IT couple working together for the first time, ten years later. It's *so juicy.*"

This time Tanner and I both roll our eyes directly at Angela.

"I'm sorry if you don't want to face the truth, but the whole reason the studio is putting so much money behind this film is because people want to see you together," Angela says. "And because Jenna got her agents to make sure this would be a closed set, we haven't released even a tidbit of info. Rumors are going to start to spread on their own. And it would be so much better if we were the ones spreading the rumors, wouldn't it?"

"You made this a closed set in your contract?" Tanner asks me directly. He seems shocked and maybe a little disappointed.

"Yeah," I say. "It's my first major role. My agent and I wanted to maintain control."

"Interesting . . ." Tanner says.

"Excuse me?" I fire back.

"Okay kids. Let's not fight." She reconsiders. "Unless you're willing to do it on camera . . ."

"No!" we both say. At least we're on the same page there.

"Wow. Alright. Calm down. Just a suggestion. Let's focus on answering some questions," Angela says. "Jenna, you first. Who have you been dating since you and Tanner broke up?"

I'm silent for a second. I don't want to go back on my decision to keep everything that happens on this set a secret. Carrie fought hard for that deal in my contract negotiations, but the last thing I want are rumors that I can't control.

Maybe Angela is right? Maybe it's better to confess a few simple facts to feed the beastly publicity machine.

"That's a lot of years to cover," I say slowly, trying to decide what to admit. "I was with Derrick Aster, the model, for two years. Other than that, no one special. I've just been focusing on my work."

"Cool, and you, Tanner?" Angela asks.

I feel my stomach drop. I realize that even ten years later I don't want to have to hear what Tanner has been up to, dating-wise. We're in the same business though, so rumors get around. I know he dated Jackie Lee, his old co-star from *The Jet*. She was actually a total sweetheart, which made it really hard to hate her after that news broke. I know that he also had an on-again off-again thing with Miley Banks who is not one or two but *eight years* younger than him, which is totally gross.

I start running through the other famous faces I've heard rumors of Tanner cuddling up to over the years, but my mind stops as he begins speaking.

"Well, after Jenna dumped me," Tanner starts.

"Me? Dump you?" I jump in. "You dumped *me!*"

His eyes go wider than I've ever seen them. "You never even talked to me. You didn't answer your phone, and I had to assume you'd broken up with me when I found your stuff gone from our apartment, because you couldn't even deal with saying the words!"

"You *cheated on me!*" I yell. "Did you actually think I was going to stay after that?"

At that, every head under the food tent turns. *Shit.* I immediately shut my mouth, but it's too late.

"Oh *please,* don't stop talking now," Angela says, clapping her hands excitedly. "This is too good."

"What's going on over here?" I hear someone say.

Walking toward us is Polly.

*Thank God.*

She's been rumored to chase publicists off her set. She'll save me.

"Nothing," Angela says feigning innocence. "Tanner and Jenna are just . . . clearing the air."

"To a publicist? I don't think so," Polly says.

I want to leap across the table and kiss her. She's just stopped an all-out war from breaking out.

Except then Polly turns her scowl from Angela to us. "Listen you two, I've worked on sets with conflict before. I've worked on sets with romance before. I don't care what's going on off camera."

Now I'm nervous. This feels more like a scolding than a saving, and I need Polly in my court. Once again Tanner has put my job in jeopardy. If he hadn't opened his big dumb mouth we could have gotten through the interview without any fireworks.

"But I do care about getting great work out of you two," Polly continues, "and about channeling your emotions to the big screen. I took this job because I remember the chemistry that Janner seemed to have. It ignited an entire country. I was dying to see if that could be transferred to these characters. Your agents both assured me that your issues were far enough in the past that they wouldn't be a problem, and I've had no reason to doubt that that's true."

She eyes us, letting us know that we better live up to her expectations. Then she smiles. "I see great energy right now. So, let's take a beat, bottle this up and save it for the fight scene we're filming this afternoon!"

Angela looks defeated. Tanner looks frustrated.

I wonder if anyone can see what I instantly feel come crawling across my face: *fear.*

I totally forgot that we were shooting the fight scene today, and now I'm legitimately worried that it's going to end with me socking Tanner right in the face.

# SIX

---

*Tanner*

FIGHT SCENES ARE USUALLY MY favorite kind of scene to shoot. They're the chance to really let loose with your character. You get to yell and scream. It's a total release of energy and stress. It's like a good workout, or better yet, a boxing match.

And the best part is, it's all just pretend.

*Usually.*

This time feels different. I'm standing across from Jenna wondering if she's actually going to punch me in the face. For the record, that's not in the script.

We're filming a scene where Jenna's character confronts my character about a receipt she found for a dinner he had at their first-date restaurant—The Landmark. There's already tension between these two, and this becomes the powder keg that sets it all off.

The logistics are simple. My character Bobby's dinner receipt says two people dined, but a week before this fight he claimed that he went alone. He said it was the only place still open after his long day of work. Of course he knows that The Landmark is their spot, he says. Then Jenna's character Grace finds out that he lied. He took a female co-worker to The Landmark. He swears he has a completely reasonable explanation, but she doesn't give a shit.

It's all feeling a little too familiar . . .

"You lied!" Jenna screams as we rehearse. "That's a betrayal!"

"I lied because I knew you'd freak out at the truth!" I yell back. "Because you don't trust me!"

"That's right, Bobby. I don't trust you because you don't deserve my trust."

"That's ridiculous! Now you're just making things up! You're using me to make excuses for all your insecurity. Why? Because your parents got divorced? Because your ex cheated? I'm not them, Grace!"

"Don't you dare bring my parents into this. This is about you. I see the way you look at other women. And I've heard rumors about what you say when I'm not around."

"You're going to blow up our relationship because of looks and rumors?"

"No. You are."

"Cut!" Polly calls out.

Her voice knocks me out of the scene. *Holy shit* that was powerful. I can't remember feeling that connected to a character, or that deep into the moment. Then again, I've never worked on something so close to my real life, with my former real life co-star. Polly's instincts that our chemistry would transform these characters were spot on.

"Shit! We need to relight," Polly says. "There's a shadow on Jenna's face. God *damnit!* That was going so well. Guys *please* do not lose this fire. Let's take two minutes."

"That won't be a problem," Jenna says, as she flips away from me. "I think I'm going to be pretty fiery anytime I think about what you said at lunch."

"You mean the truth?" I ask.

That makes her flip back.

"I think it was pretty clear that we were over in your mind when you did what you did," she says, fury blazing in her eyes. Then she stomps off. I see her tell the script coordinator that she needs to run lines. Which is a lie. We just ran them several times with no problems. She just wants to avoid me.

Once again, I feel like I'm living in a memory. Though this time we're actually *having* the fight. Ten years ago she left before listening to my side of the story.

I head over to the beverage station, grab an ice cold water and chug it. I'd like to punch something to get all my anger out, but right now I need to play it cool. And I need the crew to hurry up.

Ten excruciating minutes pass before Polly finally calls us back.

"Alright," she says. "Let's get to starting marks Tanner and Jenna. We're going to run it from the top. Still feeling feisty?"

"Oh yeah," we both say at the exact same time. I see a boom operator smirk.

*Fuck.*

Does everyone on this set know exactly what's going on here?

I realize I need to tone it down. Movie sets are like sieves for gossip. Anyone from a boom operator to the actual director can leak stuff to the press, which is exactly what Angela and her PR people want. If Jenna and I are at each other's throats now, I can't imagine how much worse it will be if news gets out that we're fighting about our break up during scripted fight scenes.

"We need to tone it down," I whisper to Jenna as we step into the scene. "People are going to start talking."

"First, that's your fault, not mine. You opened your mouth during our meeting with Angela. And second, people have been talking for ten years, Tanner. From the moment that TMI video hit the Internet."

And there it is: the infamous TMI video.

The fifteen seconds of video that ended the most real relationship I've ever had in my life.

In a freaky coincidence, it's not all that different than the dinner receipt at the center of this fake movie fight. Jenna thinks it's one thing and it's something else entirely.

God, though, if I could take it back, I would. Even now, I would.

The video that ended our relationship was staged and harmless, but it did explode on the Internet. Jenna saw it before I did, which I regret.

But what I regret more is that I let her go without fighting. I tried to find her, yes. I tried calling.

And then I stopped trying.

The first day we spoke on the set of this movie was the first time I heard her voice since our last phone call, the night before the video hit TMI.

That was ten years ago.

Hearing her mention that video right now makes my blood boil. She knew just when to drop it, too. Not when we're someplace where we can have a real conversation about what went down, but when we're surrounded by dozens of people so she can hide.

I thought I was over it, but I'm not.

Because I wasn't the only one who could have tried. She could have tried to reach out to me too. Instead she was so ready to believe that I would have messed us up, so ready to believe that she meant nothing to me. She *let* me give her up without a fight. It pisses me off to realize that she still can't admit that she gave up too.

She needs to hear it. I'm more than ready to tell her.

"Action!" Polly calls.

*Shit.* I missed my chance to respond. Suddenly we're delivering our lines in rapid fire, but I'm not focused on a single thing other than what Jenna said. It's like my mouth is performing, as my character, but my body and mind are fixated on Jenna. I cannot *wait* to say my piece once we get through this take. Luckily we fly through the lines.

"*Nice* guys!" Polly calls out. "You're really killing it today. In fact, I'd like to try something that isn't on the page. Would you be willing to add a little physicality to the scene?"

"Like one of us maybe hits the other one?" Jenna asks, her eyes sparking.

I see the same boom operator smirk again. If he isn't careful I'm going to knock him out, if Jenna doesn't knock me out first, that is.

"Ha! I was thinking more some light shoving, but let's see what we come up with. Bill, can I have you step in for a second so we can light for additional movement? Two more minutes, guys. Then we'll try this. Maybe you could run the lines with some ideas about spacing and movement while you wait."

Jenna steps out of frame, and I follow.

"I don't want to rehearse shoving you," Jenna says. "I want to save it *aalll* for the scene."

I pull her into a corner and bring her body close to mine. I want to make sure no one eavesdrops on our conversation, but Jenna is startled.

"What are you doing??" she says, pulling away.

"I could have explained that video," I say.

"You should have tried to explain a long time ago," she fires back.

"You shouldn't have run away so that I could."

The look on Jenna's face is pure rage. It's like she just watched the video all over again. She looks me dead in the eyes. "I didn't run away. I moved on."

She's angrier than I've ever seen her in my life. She might be angrier than I've ever seen *anyone*. For a moment I am legitimately afraid she's going to do something truly vicious.

Instead she turns and walks away again, this time toward the make-up station.

"Touch-up please!" she calls out to the team. She's strong and steely, nothing like the timid girl I remember.

Suddenly a strange feeling comes over me. When I look at Jenna I realize that I can't hate her. In fact, it's the total opposite.

I still want her.

I need to take a walk around the lot to cool down and get some distance, but Polly's crew is quick. We're back on our markers before I've even had a chance to figure out what the hell is going on inside my head, inside my body.

*Focus and get through it, Tanner.*

That's my mantra. This scene is five minutes long, max. I need to push through my lines. I need to remember that I'm not Tanner; I'm Bobby. And Jenna isn't Jenna; she's Grace. This is all pretend. This is all fake. My feelings are just strong because I'm really into character.

We start in on the scene. Jenna is still giving it 110 percent, and now she's adding a push here and a shove there. It all feels incredibly real.

I quickly realize that I'm going to need a new mantra.

*You're acting, Tanner. Focus on the acting.*

I try to shut down my mind and let the dialogue flow. It's memorized. I've got this.

"Now you're just making things up!" I say. "You're using me to make excuses for all your insecurity. Why? Because your parents got divorced? Because your ex cheated? I'm not them!"

"Don't you dare bring my parents into this," Jenna hisses. "This is about you. I see the way you look at other women. And I've heard rumors about what you say when I'm not around."

This time I step toward her and grab her arm after she finishes that line. My grip is tight. It startles Jenna. She pulls back quickly.

"You're going to blow up our relationship because of looks and rumors?" I say. I've said it with anger every time before, but on this take I soften my voice. I'm not asking sarcastically. I'm asking honestly.

And I'm not asking for Bobby. I'm asking for myself.

"No. You are," Jenna spits back, with feeling that's all too real.

It's painful for me to hear, but I can tell that it's equally painful for her to say.

I reach my arm back out and pull her toward me, this time softly. Then I bring her in even closer until our lips are touching and I kiss her deeply. This kiss is not like the one we had during the first scene we shot together. There's more aggression and intensity this time. My body reacts instantly. I know for a fact that if we were alone in a room right now, all our clothes would be on the floor in five seconds.

There's silence on the set when I finally release Jenna. I'm too disoriented to see at first. My head is in a fog.

Then I hear a low clap.

"Incredible kiss, you two!" Polly calls out. "But, you guys know that's not in the script, right?"

# SEVEN

*Jenna*

IT DOESN'T REALLY MATTER HOW many times I tell myself to calm down, the adrenaline keeps surging through me. I don't know how many times I circled the small set before I finally left. Vancouver is a beautiful city, but I don't see any of it. All I see is him.

I ignore the texts from my PA, grab a tea to go from a little shop I'll never be able to find again. I keep walking. Keep trying to think about anything else.

Keep thinking about nothing but him.

Tanner as Bobby. Me as Grace. My feelings in her words, her words in my mouth. I tell myself it was just acting, just a tough scene. Just transference. It meant nothing.

So then why am I still walking?

My body tells me the answer before my brain allows me to think the truth: *that kiss wasn't acting.*

It was more powerful than the first-scene kiss we shot. It was full of anger and passion. And maybe a little relief? We finally yelled and screamed some of the things we've both been holding onto for years. Scripted or not, it felt good. Maybe we *should* have talked earlier, when he'd first contacted Carrie after I signed on. It would have been awfully nice to have gotten that rage off my chest without an audience.

On the other hand, the scene was absolute perfection.

In more than one way, I think, as I absently brush a finger over my lips.

I can still feel Tanner's kiss on them. It was like we were back in that pool where we first met, introducing ourselves and kissing for the first time all over again. He felt the same. He tasted the same. And instead of pushing him away, instead of being Grace, I'd kissed him back. He felt it, too, I'm sure of it.

And that makes everything so much worse.

How was I so turned on after he grabbed me and pressed his lips against mine? Why does he still have that power over me all these years later?

I'm confused and angry with myself. This was not supposed to happen. At least when we shot the on-screen kiss in the restaurant, I'd known it was coming. I thought I had more time, but I'd still been ready for it. This time, I was caught completely off guard.

It wasn't scripted, and it wasn't expected. Here I thought he was just being an asshole, but apparently he was feeling something else entirely. Although I'm not sure what. Was he truly moved by my obvious heartache, or did he simply feel that the scene was missing something? Does he have feelings for me or was that just a choice as an actor?

And if the kiss was for me, not for my character, what does that mean?

Did the fight turn him on, or is he also feeling this weird mix-up of past and present? I need answers, but I am not about to go get them from the source. The thought of even being near Tanner right now is making my body buzz all over, in more ways than one.

In the meantime, a big glass of wine and a long chat with Walter will get me through until tomorrow. We'll come up with a plan. If nothing else, I'll feel better for talking it out instead of looping it in my head the same way I've been looping around these streets. A quick glance at the map on my phone reveals that I've wandered back toward the set, so I decide to stop by my trailer and grab tomorrow's script before heading back to the hotel.

I peer around cautiously before crossing the parking lot to my trailer. I am not in the mood to see anyone from production, but hopefully they're long gone by now. In particular, I can't stomach the idea of Angela lying in wait for me like a vulture, ready to snatch the news of our unscripted kiss like a delicious tidbit.

Once I see that the coast is clear, I bolt across the asphalt and throw open the door.

Then I scream bloody murder.

"Shit! Sorry! Hi . . ." Tanner says, frantically trying to calm me down. "Just shush a second, will you?"

I take a long inhale in, not entirely certain I'm done screaming.

"Thank you," he says, and his sincerity halts me from making any further noise for the time being. "Maybe this wasn't such a good idea. I was just afraid you wouldn't talk to me any other way."

"Correct assumption," I say, placing my hand over my still-pounding heart and trying to catch my breath. "Because I don't want to talk to you off camera. I want to maintain professional distance. I explained this on the first day." I'm terse, but how can I not be? He's in my freaking trailer! After the set has closed down. After we kissed!

For some reason, the realization that we're alone only makes my heart beat faster.

"You're right," he says earnestly. "I'm only here to apologize. Jenna, I'm sorry about what happened back there."

I'm too stunned to speak, which turns out to be a good thing because Tanner continues with even more apologies.

"I shouldn't have done that back there. Kissed you. It was unprofessional and inappropriate. Please forgive me."

"Hiding in my trailer absolutely falls into the *unprofessional and inappropriate* category, Tanner," I snip, lashing out against the feeling in my chest that's squeezing my heart. The feeling that despite all my big talk about professionalism, what I really want is to be lost in his arms, just one more time.

"I know. But your PA couldn't get ahold of you. And I got worried."

I force myself to look Tanner in the face. He looks like a guilty puppy dog—big eyes, head hung low. I did ignore a lot of texts. And regardless of how messed up the situation is between us, it was sort of nice that he wanted to make sure I got here okay.

And I want to be reasonable. Even if my insides are all wrecked from the past, we still have the present to work through together. Maybe if I raise the white flag we'll actually get through this thing in one piece.

I sit down next to Tanner, just to let him know I'm not planning on shoving him straight out of my trailer anymore. And then I dig deep and play nice. "Obviously our bodies have some sort of muscle memory. We're just reacting to that. It doesn't mean anything."

He laughs. "Yeah. I guess that makes sense."

"Also that was totally in the heat of a big scene moment. Good actors let themselves get carried away. That's what happened. We can still be adults about this, moving forward. We can still be professional."

"Right, right. We're professionals."

He's looking at me now. I can't quite make out the expression on his face.

Part of me hopes he's as confused as I am.

"Today meant nothing," I say. "Our past is in the past."

"Totally in the past. But when I'm working with you . . ."

I feel myself inch closer to him. " . . . what?"

"Sometimes I can't tell where we leave off and our characters begin."

Is he sitting nearer than he was a few seconds ago?

"I know. I feel the same way," I confess, and then I'm definitely moving closer to him. Definitely staring at his lips. We're like two magnets. Simply telling them to stay apart never stops the pull.

"But that's the job, right?" he says, and his eyes are on my mouth now.

I nod. "We have to put everything aside and just focus on the work."

"Right. Yes. I can do that." He's so close we're almost touching. Then he reaches his hand out and places it on my thigh. I feel a chill run up my body, and I close my eyes. The warm, heavy feeling of his hand is so familiar and so exciting at once. "Can *you* do that?"

The honest answer is I don't know. I open my eyes and find him staring at me. I get lost in his stare. For a moment, we hesitate.

Then the next thing I know, my lips are pressed against his and his tongue is finding its way inside my mouth. I don't know who started it, but neither of us can deny this is what we both want in this moment. Have wanted since this afternoon. Maybe since we first saw each other outside craft services two weeks ago.

He cradles my face between his hands and shifts me closer, as though afraid I'll break our connection.

But I'm not going anywhere. I want more. I swing my leg over to straddle him, so I can press my hips into his pelvis. I groan when I feel how hard he is, groan with the need that's already built up unbearably between my thighs. I rock back and forth, desperate. Only a few scraps of cloth stand between us, but they're enough to frustrate me.

He stands up, me still astride him, then he tosses me onto my back in front of him. He kneels on the ground, and I'm lying on the couch of my trailer looking up at the ceiling, and a part of me is wondering how the hell this happened again. But a much louder part of me doesn't want it to end before we're both naked and screaming out all our unresolved anger in orgasm.

Before I have time to register what's happening, I feel Tanner's fingers creep up my thighs and under my panties. He plays with me, teasing before he plunges two fingers inside my body.

I gasp in surprise and delight.

*This. This is what I need.*

I let my thighs fall farther apart, giving him all the access he wants. Tanner dances and swirls his fingers around, first deep inside me and then up to brush my clit. I grip the couch, nearly paralyzed in anticipation. My legs begin to shake, and I can't remember my own name anymore. All I can think about is how incredible this feels, and how, improbably, he's become even more talented at touching a woman over the years. *Holy shit.*

I've never been fingered like this before.

He leaves one hand to work every centimeter of my clit then takes the other and dances it up and down the inside of my thighs until I'm crying out. His free hand covers my mouth, but that doesn't help. It isn't until he stills that I quiet, although my hips are still rocking greedily, trying to get what I want from his fingers.

"Sshh," he says, "Someone might still be around."

"I don't care," I moan, and, in the moment, I swear I don't. Let everyone hear how glorious this is. Tanner grins as he presses his fingers back inside me, bending them and twisting them, showing off more moves that get my body pulsing and my pussy soaking wet.

I'm going to come. I'm so close. "Fuck, Tanner, yes . . ."

"Yes," he growls, and that's all it takes to send me flying over the edge into ecstasy.

. . . just as someone knocks on the trailer door.

Tanner's hand goes back over my mouth, and I bite down on my cheek to contain my moan as the last few aftershocks rack my body. He stares at me, helping me come down, our bodies rocking together as I slowly stop convulsing.

"Hello? Jenna?" a voice calls from outside. It's one of the production assistants. "If you're there, Polly was hoping to re-shoot a few lines before we wrap for the day," she says. "Can you be on set in five? And do you have any idea where Tanner is?"

But the more important question at the moment is, what the hell just happened?

# EIGHT

*Tanner*

FOR THE FIRST TIME IN my life I don't want to hear my director call it a wrap for the day.

Normally I'm just going through the motions at this point, my mind more focused on the ESPN and cold beer awaiting me than on turning in an Oscar-worthy performance. Now, though, as we're winding down on those last shots that Polly needed, I'm actually considering flubbing my lines to eat up more time.

Although it could happen even without me doing it on purpose, considering the kind of shape I'm in.

It took me fifteen minutes to get through this one scene—that we'd already shot once earlier today—because my mind was so all over the place. And my body. I'm pretty sure I walked onto the set fully hard.

I can't stop thinking about what happened in Jenna's trailer. About what we did. About what *I* did. Can't stop thinking about her pussy pulsing around my fingers and her beautiful face when she came—she's as gorgeous as I remembered when she's lost in orgasm, and the ache in my balls has me wanting to see that look again real soon.

But the ache in my stomach that says I really screwed things up is much worse than any pain below the waist.

We were just starting to talk to each other again. Starting to work things out. Somehow I have a feeling this is not what Jenna meant when she said she wanted to keep things professional.

And, fuck! What if we'd been caught?

That's just what Jenna needs—a story about us fooling around to get spread around by one underpaid crewmember and suddenly TMI is blasting too much information once again.

It was a mistake. I know it was. I need to apologize to Jenna. Only, without a single minute to process what happened back there, I don't know what to say.

We run through our shots, my mind spinning the whole time.

Jenna's barely looked at me except when she's had to for the scene. I assume she's angry, and she has every right to be. It must seem like I came to her trailer under false pretenses. And I didn't. I didn't plan that I would end up all but fucking her.

That has to be part of my apology. I have to make sure I explain that I really did go to her trailer to set things right between us. The rest just . . . happened.

And unless I'm reading things totally wrong, she wanted it, too. She moved toward me. She let me touch her.

*God she felt good.*

"Cut!" Polly yells. "That's it for today. You can get back to whatever you were doing before I rudely interrupted you."

*Shit.* Did Polly just look our way? Did someone actually see us? Or, more likely, hear us?

Am I just being paranoid?

I look over at Jenna, wondering if she picked up on the same comment from Polly. Somehow she's already over with her wardrobe person getting out of costume. She looks rattled and uncomfortable. My stomach sinks. She regrets what we did, she'll never speak to me as anyone but Grace again. I can practically see it all.

Then it hits me exactly why she's probably so upset: *Walter.* Jenna has a fucking boyfriend.

Now I have regrets. Big regrets.

Shit.

My need to apologize gets even more urgent, in light of this. If I were her, I'd be feeling overwhelmed and angry too. If I were *him*, I'd kill me. The irony doesn't escape me, by the way, that the most famous victim of infidelity since Jennifer Aniston just cheated. With me.

I need to clear the air. This time nowhere near a confined space with a couch.

I snag Jenna before she's anywhere near her trailer. This time, we're in a well-lit section of the lot where lots of people are passing by. No one is close enough to listen to our conversation. It's perfect, except for my nerves. I'm damn near shaking as I touch her arm to ask if we can talk. It doesn't help that she jumps almost a mile the minute my arm grazes her skin.

"Hey, I want to apologize, for real this time. That was totally unprofessional, and I'm really sorry," I say quietly. "That wasn't my intention when I came to your trailer. I honestly just wanted to clear the air."

Jenna nods. She's agreeing, but she doesn't seem pissed. She actually looks relieved.

"Good. I was hoping you'd feel that way. That can *never* happen again. It's too risky." I notice her nervously fidget with her fingers.

"Yes. Exactly. Completely agreed. Never again."

"Okay. Cool. Well . . . Great." Now Jenna shifts on her feet and touches her hair.

"So are you going to tell your boyfriend about it?"

"What boyfriend? I don't have a boyfriend."

"Oh," I say, confused. "I guess I got that mixed up."

"Yeah, you did. I definitely don't have a boyfriend."

She sneaks a quick look up and directly at me before jutting her eyes down and away. I used to call it her French eyes. The move made me feel like I was in some black and white French romance flick . . . or vintage French porn. When we first met that look could get me hard in a hot second.

Turns out, it still can.

We're quiet for a moment. I don't know what she's thinking, but

I'm turning this new information over in my head. Maybe he was just a friend with benefits. Or an uncle I don't remember.

So where does that leave me?

I look at her and she's looking at me, and this time we both cut our eyes away.

"Even though I'm sorry," I venture, "I don't regret it." More silence, but only for a moment.

"It *was* pretty hot," she agrees, and even without glancing over, I can hear the smile in her voice.

"We're shooting Seven next," she says conversationally. Seven is the first time that Bobby and Grace go home together. Despite a no-nudity clause in Jenna's contract, the scene looks to be pretty steamy. There will be tons of shots of our bare skin, sliding against each other, shots of neck kissing and hair pulling and all the other things I've been fantasizing about doing to her off-camera.

"So, do you maybe want to get together tonight to rehearse it before we shoot Monday?" I ask.

I didn't really mean to say that out loud. I feel like some weird demon took control of my mouth. The words just came flying out like some kind of physical reaction. And now I can't take them back.

But then Jenna says, "Yes, definitely," without a single bit of hesitation.

*Play it cool, Tanner. Roll with it.*

"Okay good. Yeah. Cool. My room?" Not sure that was "cool" but it was certainly bold. She's smiling, and either I'm crazy or it's a flirty grin.

"I don't know. Do you have a suite?"

Yep, definitely flirty. Game on, Jenna Stahl. "I do. Room 1019. King suite. Come see if it's up to your lead actress standards." I wink at her, and am gratified to see her blush. I can't wait to see the flush on her cheeks when I make her come again, this time with my mouth.

Wait. That's not what I'm supposed to be thinking about. Are we still talking about rehearsing?

"Deal. Your room. Nine o'clock?" She pivots to leave, hardly waiting for my answer. Like it would be anything other than acquiescence.

And it is. "Yeah. Perfect. See you then."

I watch her ass as she walks away, this time without a measure of guilt.

And with that I can't decide if this late night rehearsal is the best or worst idea I've ever had.

By ten after nine, when Jenna is nowhere to be found, I've decided it's definitely the worst. I pick up the remote and head for the minibar, ready to drown my feelings in a combination of tequila and basketball.

Then there's a knock on the door.

"Hi, I'm sorry I'm late," Jenna says breezily as she walks in, oblivious to my gaping.

At least, that's what I think she said. I can't focus on anything but the thin white T-shirt she's wearing over a black lace bra. It shows off every curve of her perfect breasts. I force myself to think of something cold and boring—*miserable icy showers at Aunt Pat's beach house!*—and I'm saved, for now.

"No worries," I say, recovering quickly. "Something to drink?"

"No thanks," Jenna says. Then she takes the script out of her bag and starts leafing through the pages. "Do you wanna get your script?"

"Oh. Yeah. Sure. Of course." I escape into my bedroom to grab it, and mentally slap myself across the face. *She's here to work, idiot.*

"I think we should use your kitchen counter as the bar," Jenna calls from the other room.

"Fine," I say as I walk back in, script in hand.

"It's a little bright in here. Mind if I dim the lights?"

I want to say *No, Jenna, if you dim the lights then this is going to feel too much like a real bar, and in a real bar I wouldn't make it through a single line. I'd just throw you up on the counter and fuck your brains out.*

But instead I nod a yes. I feel like I'm hanging on by a thread, and desperately hoping she doesn't notice.

"K, you lean on the counter opposite me," Jenna directs. "Let's take it from the top of page twenty-five."

I move in like she suggested, then scan the page. The dialogue seems harmless enough. Grace and Bobby are chatting after they've met up at happy hour after a long day of work. It's friendly and simple.

"You start," I say.

"Right . . ."

There is a little tone of hesitation in Jenna's response—like she isn't sure about something. But what? I look up from my script and find her staring at me. Why? Is she nervous or uncomfortable? Does she not know how to approach this scene? Or is she doing something to get into character?

Whatever it is, she needs to stop because it's making me crazy. With her leaning, I can't help but stare directly at that black bra peeking through her shirt, and the big, round breasts pressing up against the fabric. *Fuck.* I can see the outline of her nipples, hard in the air-conditioning, and my cock jumps in response.

Finally, Jenna starts. "How was your day, love?"

I have to look down to read my line, thank God. "Eh. Fine. I missed you."

She takes a step toward me. "AAww, what did you miss about me?"

I look down for my next line, then I notice that's not what she was supposed to say. Grace is supposed say, "That's sweet."

My throat suddenly feels tight and the air, electric.

"Where do I start?" I ask, thinking about how much I've missed the smell of her on my pillows and seeing her favorite coffee mug in my sink every morning, and staying up late to watch bad television while cheating on our diets with a bag of microwave popcorn.

I decide to keep the discussion on a physical level. That's what she wants to hear.

I close the space between us at the counter and move my arm back behind her. Jenna looks down at my arm then her fingers reach over and touch the muscles around my biceps. She curls her lips, giving me an almost angry glare.

"Start somewhere good. You've got a lot of making up to do."

The edge in her voice makes my dick throb.

"I missed your perfect ass," I say.

"Not good enough," Jenna replies.

"I missed the sound of you moaning for more, like when I fingered you inside your trailer."

"Like this?" Jenna asks, and then leans over and moans in my ear, shooting a pulse up and down my entire body. "Do you want more of that?"

I nod then grab her hand and place it on my dick so she can feel how hard she has me.

"Well then, there are some things I want too."

There is an intensity in Jenna's eyes that I've never seen before. They're narrow and pointed in a sexy, devilish way. It makes me want to pick her up, run her over to the giant king bed and throw her down. Instead, she makes the first move. She closes her fingers around my shirt and pulls me in closer.

"Fuck me, Tanner," she says. "Show me how much you've missed me."

I take my hands and cradle her face then kiss her deeply. All those hours of pent-up energy I've been holding find their outlet in her as she tangles her tongue with mine.

I grab her around the waist and lift her up onto the counter. The thin fabric of her shorts gives easily, as I rip it right down the seam. She squeals in surprise, and I grin. I toss the now-useless scrap on the floor and pull her panties down her thighs, leaving her to kick them off as I dive forward, intent on my goal. She's wet already, and I'm eager to taste her glistening liquid, to lick it clean off her slit. But first I run my tongue up and down her thighs, gently.

"Hurry," she urges, and I comply.

When my tongue delves in and up her smooth inner lips, I'm not sure which one of us moans louder. She still tastes like strawberries. She still tastes like heaven.

Aware of her urgency, I don't savor this moment the way I want to, instead, I use my tongue to bring her to the edge of orgasm as quickly as I can, until she's begging me for release, for just one more lick to send her flying.

And then I don't.

The Earth is going to shatter when I let her come, which means putting it off once or twice first. I stand up and move to rip the T-shirt off Jenna's body, but she's one step ahead of me.

"God, Jenna," I say as I take in the perfect shape of her round breasts. They're so full, so luscious. I want them in my hands, *now*. I slide both my hands up her stomach and cup them as I kiss her again, this time sharing her taste with her.

"I need you," she says, pulling back from my mouth, and then she jumps into my arms, straddling my body with her strong legs, her warm pussy pressing against my dick. I'm so hard that just the thought of what's about to happen has me on the edge, and she knows it, squirming against me and moaning in my ear.

I walk us both over to the bed and lower her down on the mattress. I'm ready for another taste of her, but she stops me by grabbing my face. Then she flips us over so that I'm pinned down between her legs at my middle and arms at my chest.

"My turn," she says. Then she unbuttons my shirt and pants, peeling them both off in a matter of seconds. I reach out to feel the searing heat of her skin against my fingers, but she's already moving out of my reach.

I groan in frustration, but when I feel her hand wrap around my shaft, I'm groaning for an entirely different reason.

"Hard and fast," she says, bending down to swirl her tongue around my crown.

"But—" I start to protest, wanting to take my time, wanting to finish teasing her.

And then the next thing I know she has my cock deep inside her mouth. I feel my whole body throb as I let out a long growl.

*Holy shit.*

Jenna has not lost any skills in the blowjob department. She was always a master and right now her tongue is doing things that are going to make me explode. And when she takes me inside her throat? I swear I see stars.

Suddenly, though, she stops.

I'm still panting from the feeling of her lips around my dick, my vision still blurry from the near orgasm. "What happened?" I ask.

"I can't wait any longer," she says. And then she crawls up and over me until she's sitting so she can guide my cock inside her body. She's tight and hot as I slide in. We both hiss at the moment I'm completely inside, filling and stretching her. Talk about seeing stars. I'm in fucking ecstasy. I'm fucking home.

She sits there for a moment, still, adjusting. Then she finally starts moving, and she lets everything loose. Weeks—no years—of tension seemed to be released as she writhes and moans and screams.

I'm hypnotized by her. It feels so good to be inside her, to have her riding my dick, and yet I'm truly mesmerized watching her. It's the best part of what's happening now. Seeing her like this, so full of passion and maybe even rage, takes me to a place that I haven't been in, well, maybe ever.

She's so beautiful on top of me, head thrown back as she rides me to the place she wants to be. So angry when I torture her, holding her hands away so she can't rub her clit. But when, at last, I take mercy and use my thumb to draw small, tight circles on that bundle of nerves until she seizes up around me and the vice grip of her pussy makes me come too, hard and furiously, that's when it hits me.

I'm still in love with Jenna Stahl.

# NINE

---

*Jenna*

I REMEMBER WHERE I AM before my eyes open and wonder if the safest thing to do is keep them closed.

Waking up means all of this really happened.

I am really in bed with Tanner James.

I really spent all night having hot, dirty sex with him before we collapsed next to each other, too worn out to move.

This was obviously not my best decision—who jumps back into bed with the man who broke her heart once before?

I sneak one eye open a peek just to be 100 percent sure. It catches Tanner's tan, muscular shoulder just where it meets his hulking chest, and I feel a fresh wave of desire roll down my body, making me want to jump on top of him all over again. I've been trying to forget what it's like to have Tanner James inside me for the better part of a decade, and now I have to start all over again, because the answer is *really fucking good.*

No. The answer is *the fucking best.*

And last night was better than even the hottest nights we'd had in the past. I'm so confused right now—what am I doing? I went from cutting him off to seducing him in the span of two weeks. I can blame my libido, or the old feelings from the past bubbling to the surface. But another part of me is wondering what if? What if we . . . ?

But no, of course there won't be a *we*. It's impossible.

Although *we* certainly had some very compelling orgasms last night . . .

Even the thought of it prompts a very familiar pulsing in between my legs. If I stay in this bed a second longer I will have no control over what happens next. And that won't go any further toward untangling my thoughts and feelings about what all this means for Tanner and I.

I slide out of bed and pad to the other room to throw on my clothes. Tanner is still sound asleep, though he murmurs something I can't understand as I ease the door open. I don't know if he'll be offended or relieved that I snuck out, but it's what I'm doing. I'll have to face him eventually, but when I can't avoid conflict entirely, I will definitely take procrastination if available.

I stop by my room for the world's quickest shower and change before heading downstairs. The lobby doors open onto crisp Canadian air, and my head already feels clearer.

I catch a sly smile from the valet and wonder if he remembers me walking in with Tanner last night after leaving the set. I can get by without being instantly noticed when I'm by myself, but every single person in this town—if not this world—would recognize Tanner James. He's an international superstar. People are dying to catch him with a brand new girl, especially if she happens to be the old girl. Put us together, and we're instantly recognizable.

At least, we used to be.

Trying to clear my mind, I smile back, slip the valet a tip and jump into my rental car.

I have no particular destination in mind, just a vague idea about finding a tea, a park, a quiet place to think.

The first few blocks are bliss. I fly by a few shops and cafes as they're just starting to open for the day. I see a few locals taking their Goldendoodles and French bulldogs for a morning stroll. A few joggers are braving a run along the hilly streets for a morning sweat. I wonder if I can re-discover the cute little coffee shop from my walk. Slowing the car,

I look for familiar landmarks.

Unfortunately, the one I find isn't the one I want.

I'm right across from a spot called The Hot Griddle Café . . . the exact same name as an LA spot where Tanner and I ate pancakes the morning after our first time together. We'd sat next to each other in a booth, unable to be even as far apart as across the table. Hot coffee and maple syrup tasted like desire to me for months after.

And with that my blissfully clear mind is jam-packed full of the thoughts I'd meant to be avoiding: *How could last night be so good after what Tanner did to me? Could we really go back to how it was in the beginning after he cheated? Should we talk about the video? It was just a kiss. Was our whole relationship worth throwing away for one kiss?*

*What if he's right and I ran away too soon?*

I give up on the little shop and park, walking into the first Tim Horton's for a quick cup of chai and a yogurt. I jot them both down, hoping the combination of caffeine and protein will lead to the kind of mental clarity I'm seeking, but to no avail. Maybe there *are* no good answers, I think, as I toss my trash in the bin and push open the door.

But on my way to the car I have the strange feeling that I'm being followed. I pick up my speed and try to see if there's a person trailing me in the window of one of the shops near Walfred. No luck. I slow down a tad, wondering if I'll be able to hear real footsteps, but I can't make them out against the music blaring from a nearby car. So I take the risk and turn around.

*Snap.*

I'm shot with the bright light of a camera flash. Fucking paparazzi. This guy is tall and thin with dark hair and a serious five o'clock shadow for this early in the morning. He looks like most of the rest—disheveled and hungry for blood.

I cover my face knowing they'll never be able to sell an obscured shot and dash toward my car. He follows, snapping away, but I win out, hop in and speed off.

There's only one possible way to salvage my morning if I plan to be any good on set this afternoon, and as soon as I'm in my hotel room,

I pull out my laptop and connect to the Internet.

"Why on earth are you Skyping me before noon on a weekend?" Walter asks grouchily as he rubs his eyes.

"Because I fucked Tanner last night," I reply.

"And I'm awake," he says, moving off-camera for a moment and reappearing in his favorite kimono with a can of Red Bull.

Even from miles and miles away, Walter saves me. He insists I call down to room service for an immediate Bloody Mary and directs me to put on one of the lavender-infused facemasks that he slipped into my suitcase before I left LA. I am now slightly calmer.

Walter, on the other hand, is in what he would call "a tizzy."

"Think you have enough booze in you to discuss the fact that you walked out on Tanner instead of facing the music, Missy?"

Now I'm not so sure that calling Walter was the best idea.

"What was I supposed to do?" I couldn't think straight with a Greek god next to me in bed.

"Not cower like such a fucking conflict avoider, like you *always* do."

"I wasn't avoiding conflict. I was avoiding fucking my co-star/ex-boyfriend for the third time in six hours."

"Third?"

"We did it twice. Once in the bed, once in the shower."

Walters fan himself dramatically. "Hold on. I need a minute to live vicariously through your sex life because mine is a barren wasteland." He takes a deep breath, his eyes closed, a smile perched on his lips. Then he reopens his eyes. "Okay. Go on."

"I was saying, what was my option given the situation? But now I need to make it clear this fling is not going to become a *thing*."

"One fuck fest does not a relationship make, Jenna."

"But it starts there. And next thing I know, I'm in deep all over again. Since when has anyone been able to have casual sex with an ex without getting feelings involved?"

"Valid point."

"So this has to be a one-shot deal. If it turns into a regular activity, I'm not going to be able to handle it. And the second time my heart gets broken by him, I'll only have myself to blame."

"What makes you so sure about that? I mean I'm the last person who should defend shacking up with an ex—because I've done it so many times and we both know how that's worked out—but, I should not be used as an example for anything. You guys were so young when you were together. I sure as shit made some mistakes at that age I'll always regret. What if you're Tanner's one big regret?"

My heart gives a little jump at the thought, and I sternly tell it to stop. I'm only second-guessing the past because I want to believe that I can trust Tanner now. But wanting something to be true doesn't make it so. And if I'd been wrong about the extent of his cheating, he surely would have cleared things up a long time ago.

"I know Tanner," I say to Walter, hoping he won't probe any further. "And I know I can't trust him with my heart ever again. I will literally not survive a break up like we went through last time around."

"I hear you on that," Walter says with a raise of his own cocktail glass. Walter is of the strong opinion that no one should ever drink alone, even on the phone. "But I have to say, I disagree. Sort of."

I pause, confused. What could he possibly disagree with?

"See, I'm looking at you with your cute little morning-after glow, and confidence in your face I haven't seen in a very long time. Would just the sex alone really be that bad? If you already have your mind completely made up that you can't trust him, you're in a lot less danger of falling for him again."

I'm quiet for a moment, considering. I see where he's coming from, and the thought of more sex definitely isn't terrible. In fact, it's the opposite of terrible. That leaves just the question of trust. I know I can't trust Tanner, and this scenario makes that a non-issue, but can I trust myself not to get emotional?

"I'm not going to lie—sex with Tanner is so insanely amazing that it's actually making me consider this. When I was with him last night, I felt more powerful and wanted than I have in years. Maybe you're right. Maybe I *do* need that confidence right now. Does that sound crazy? Is that using him?"

"Yes, but in a good way. He'll be using you too. It all works out."

"Maybe it could even help me with the role," I say, but as I do, another thought enters my mind. It's a little devilish, and a little selfish, and I know Walter will eat it right up. "Honestly," I confess, "I might not have it as good as Tanner ever again. Don't I deserve the best sex of my life for just a few months? And then at the end, I get to be the one to walk away like the whole thing was no big deal."

"Now you're getting messy and risky," Walter warns. "I'm starting to have second thoughts. Let me mull it over a bit more. Now, tell me the real business—any cute guys in Wardrobe or Makeup that I need to fly out and meet?"

I spend the next quarter of an hour entertaining Walter with tales from the set, then I wrap things up in time to get ready for my call time. We're in the middle of goodbyes when my phone pings with a message.

It's from Tanner.

.

I smile a devilish smile.

"Do not reply to that text that is clearly from Tanner without my approval!" Walter commands.

"Don't worry," I say, "I'm not going to reply at all. Not until I'm sure about what happens next."

After I hang up with Walter, I throw on the hotel's fabulously plush terrycloth robe, pull my hair into a ponytail, and then settle onto the chaise in the sitting area for a little brainstorming session with the black and white striped notebook my mom gave me for a birthday gift.

On the top of a blank page I write: *New Rules for Tanner and Jenna*.

I look at the headline, then tear out that page and start over.

This time I write: *New Rules for Jenna*.

Tanner James is not going to control my life again. This time, I'm going to be the one in the driver's seat.

# TEN

*Tanner*

THERE'S NO WAY IN HELL *Jenna is going to be here when I open my eyes*. That was the last thought I had before I fell asleep. I usually love being right.

Not this time.

I ended up spending the better part of the morning lounging around the hotel room wasting a shitload of time flipping through the movie channels. Finally I gave up on the idea that Jenna might come back and hit the gym. I thought about nothing else during my time on the treadmill, nor during my weights, and by the time I got back up to my shower, I was eaten up with need.

I jerked off in the shower, but it wasn't anywhere close to the real thing.

Afterward I texted her, but got no response. But then, I'd understand if she was freaking out. After all, so far every single time she's drawn a line, we've hopped right over it. Or in the case of last night, fucked it out of existence altogether.

I pull on a pair of Calvins and flip through the room service menu, idly thinking about eggs. Idly thinking about Jenna. She used to love a posh hotel room, and she lived for room service.

"What could possibly be more decadent than eating in bed, and not being the one to clean up the crumbs after?" she'd always said. "This is how to *live*."

And boy, did we used to live.

Jenna and I used to have a ridiculous tradition of ordering two breakfasts apiece and then sharing, creating our own little buffet so we wouldn't have to leave our bubble. At first, between her modeling gigs in New York, Paris, and London, plus my shooting schedule, there were months where the only time we saw each other was for a 48-hour fling in a hotel room followed by that gargantuan breakfast. Toward the end, that had changed, but the tradition remained. Jenna used to say that we had the kind of sex that worked off enough calories to make our heaping platefuls null and void.

She was right.

Last night was maybe even a tad conservative for us, only going two rounds instead of the four we could do a decade ago. But we were younger then. Still, I wouldn't mind the challenge.

I glance at my phone about five more times, giving her plenty of chances to remember that we should be eating right about now, but she never texts back. I start multiple messages inviting her to breakfast, but I delete every one. I don't want to be desperate.

So instead I just order one breakfast. And I limit the carbs. And I'm bummed.

As I wait for my western omelet with a side of fruit, I vow to stop fiddling with my phone and finally tune back in to what's on the TV: fucking TMI. A pang hits my stomach like a quick gut punch. TMI is the show that ended my relationship with Jenna. If I were the kind of guy who believed in signs, I'd say this is definitely one—but would it be good or bad?

Would this be my cue to finally tell her the truth from back then, or a message saying that it's already over before it's begun? And was last night an indication that something new truly *has* begun? I don't want to presume, especially with the unanswered text situation, but I can't imagine that we won't find ourselves in bed together again. And again.

And then what?

My mind finally flips away from thoughts of what's next with Jenna, but it heads over to the memory of what happened ten years ago.

I was on set with the sequel to *The Jet* in LA while Jenna was walking fall Fashion Week in Manhattan. It was one of those long stretches where we were apart. We'd been apart a lot that summer and into the fall. She'd booked a giant contract with Marissa's Closet and started flying around the world to shoot lingerie ads in what felt like every castle in Europe. I was stuck in LA training for the next installment of the movie.

Both of us were frustrated with the constant distance, but I had the sense Jenna was also jealous. I got it. I would have been too, if I'd been in her shoes. She'd confessed to me that she wanted to act early on in our relationship, and I think it was getting harder and harder for her to see me in the world she wanted but couldn't yet have. Modeling is impossible as is, but she was half in that world and half in mine. I knew she preferred my lifestyle to her own, and I knew it was hard to just be the girl on the arm of some movie superhero that people were fawning over for no reason. I felt bad for her.

But I was frustrated with her, too. She was frequently turning down opportunities to audition so she could be with me, so she could be part of *my* movie lifestyle instead of building one of her own. I didn't argue with her about it—of course I didn't, she never let us have a conversation that was at all heated—but there was an underlying tension that seemed to bleed into our days away from each other. I wanted her with me, but I didn't want her with me if it was taking her away from her dreams. So sometimes I made excuses that I was too busy to see her, hoping she'd take a bit part or book a role that might lead to something bigger. More often than not, she just felt like I was pushing her away.

It didn't help that my publicists wanted me out every night of the week. Apparently the producers were nervous about launching the sequel in a year already hyper-crowded by comic-book movies. They needed me to be as visible as possible to help drive people to the theater.

"People don't go see movies," I remember the head publicist at the time saying, "They go see movie stars."

I'll be honest. I was riding high with the thrill of being that star. I'd hit the sweet spot where guys want to be you and girls want to screw you—Celebrity Magic, my agents explained. I couldn't risk losing that momentum, especially with a huge movie on the line.

That was where my head was when Natalia Lowen approached me about the kiss-cam charity event. I was thinking about my career, not my relationship. I was thinking about my job.

The setup was innocent enough. Pairs of celebs were selected to compete against each other in an on-camera kissing contest for a big cash prize they would ultimately donate to the charity of their choice. At the time I'd just started working with St. Anselm's Children's Hospital, so this felt like a great way to start the relationship off on the right foot.

Of course, that meant I *had* to win the contest.

And winning meant being one half of the hottest kiss among twelve sets of celebs.

I was paired with Natalia, which did not help matters when it came to Jenna ultimately finding out. Natalia was a model who had successfully transitioned into acting—living Jenna's dream. She was also smoking hot, objectively speaking, and the opposite of Jenna looks-wise. Natalia had blond hair to Jenna's deep brown, and blue eyes to Jenna's green. But that's not where my mind was when I agreed to kiss her for this dumb charity.

Her looks weren't anything I thought twice about, because the most beautiful girl in the world was already mine.

I specifically asked if the shot was going to be on TV, and the crew that approached Natalia said *no*.

That was a lie.

Actually, the whole thing was a lie. There wasn't a kissing contest. There wasn't even a charity event. The film crew were just pranksters who'd convinced Natalia they were doing a good deed so they could get scandalous celebrity footage and sell it for top dollar to TMI.

Not only did it air on TMI's primetime show before I had the chance to explain the whole charade to Jenna, but also it looked completely like I was kissing Natalia for real.

It was all over their website too. *Is Janner over?! Tanner James makes out with Natalia Lowen while Jenna Stahl is lonely in New York.* They paired the really hot kissing video—when I make it good, I make it good—with footage caught of Jenna walking alone, makeup-less, wearing sweats and a ragged sweatshirt I used to wear in high school. It made her look lonely and pathetic. It was brutal and deceiving.

I later tried to get TMI to air my rebuttal, but no one wanted to pick up my side of the story. Cheating scandals earn more viewers than misguided attempts at raising money for charity. That film crew, whoever they were, knew just what would sell. They orchestrated the whole event perfectly.

And I fell for it, hook, line, and sinker. I *had* to be the best. I *had* to win. So I really went for it with Natalia. The footage of me kissing her looks incredibly real.

I would have believed it were real if I were Jenna.

Within hours of the video hitting the Internet it was absolutely everywhere, including Jenna's phone. I tried to call her, but she wouldn't answer my calls. When I wrapped *The Jet* sequel a few days later and got to our apartment, she'd moved out.

I had another shoot right away back home in Australia—a movie I'd been looking forward to because I'd get to be back home for a period of time for the first time in years. The timing with the video was the worst. I was pissed that I was too busy to deal with it. I was pissed that Jenna knew my schedule was crammed and still wouldn't answer my calls. I was pissed that she'd given up on us so easily, so I decided to just give myself a few days to cool off before I tried to figure out how to best reach her. Then I heard through the grapevine that she'd booked a spot as a judge on a reality show. Even mad as I was, I was excited for her. It wasn't the acting break she wanted, but it was *something*. It was a beginning. I'd been out of her life barely two weeks, and she'd landed her first real non-modeling gig.

That's when I realized I had to let her go.

I told my friends I didn't have time to keep chasing her and stay focused on my acting. The truth was I believed *she* didn't have time for our relationship and her career. She'd been giving up so much for me, and if I explained the truth about the video to her, she'd go right back to sacrificing again.

So she ran, but I let her go.

I let her go, and I don't regret my reasons, but I regret losing her.

And I regret that she thinks I cheated on her, that I would ever hurt her like that. I want to punch the smarmy host right in the TV screen about now. And then find those asshole pranksters that set me up for the Kiss Cam charade and punch them. And then maybe even chew out Natalia for being so gullible.

But I know I should be kicking myself in the ass, too. I'm not only responsible for what happened that day, but I'm also responsible for what happened after. For losing her. For losing us.

I just kept thinking I'd find an opportunity to make it right, but I never did.

And the worst part is that it was all for nothing. Even stepping away, her career hasn't blossomed the way it should have. The way I hoped it would. So, when Three Spot Films took me up on my suggestion to co-produce a Janner reunion film, I knew they agreed because of the money that could be made from the publicity. But I put together this opportunity because it was time for the world to see the star Jenna was meant to be. And because I was tired of waiting for the universe to offer me a second chance. This time, I made my own chance, and I'm determined not to screw it up.

I don't have any scenes on the shooting schedule for today, but I decide to head to set anyway. When you're in production mode and away from home, there isn't much else to do. I can't risk heading to the beach; I might get a sunburn and the make-up department would rake me over the coals. I'd rather not hang around town because paparazzi will probably swarm with questions about filming. And there's also the fact that Jenna is on set . . . shooting a scene where she works out with her character's best friend . . . wearing what I can only imagine are skin-tight spandex pants and a sports bra.

I find a spot to successfully hide out and watch while Jenna and Kit shoot the scene. I'm pretty sure the camera guy hiding me knows exactly what's up, but I don't give a shit. He has an even better view of Jenna in action.

I was right—the wardrobe is skintight black spandex pants and a hot yellow sports bra. Jenna looks fucking amazing. And she's doing an amazing job. I can't take my eyes off her in this scene. She's a natural, like I always told her she would be. Watching her I'm filled with this weird sense of pride—like that's *my* Jenna getting it done out there. It feels good to have that connection to her again. It feels good to be around her every day again.

Why the fuck did I wait so long to try to make things right?

That decision makes zero sense as I stand here now, eyes fixed on the gorgeous, perfect girlfriend I let get away all those years ago. I don't want to lose her again. And I definitely don't want to lose the chance to feel myself deep inside her over and over and over.

Maybe that's where I'll start, and maybe I can appeal to the new actor in her. I can convince her that if we keep having sex it will be good for character chemistry.

Is that conniving?

A little.

But it's a necessary means to a beautiful end. At least that's what I'm telling myself as I prepare to chat with Jenna after her scene. I'll casually stroll up to her in the crafty tent and tell her I just came to set to pick up something from my trailer. Then I'll just as casually propose this little plan.

To my surprise it's Jenna who finds *me* near the taco truck fifteen minutes later. She walks right up. There's a determined glare in her eyes, which can only mean one thing—It's "never again" spiel time.

But I'm prepared to cut her off and change the game. I've got my own spiel.

"Hey," Jenna says with a smile that totally throws me off. "I didn't expect to see you on set. I'm glad you came. Did you see my scenes? I think it went well."

"Uh . . ." She's so easygoing. So laidback that I nearly forget my lines. "Yeah. I did. I came to grab something and I caught the last few takes."

"Oh good." She brushes her hair behind her ear. And did she just take a step closer? "I was actually going to head back to your hotel room later if you weren't on set."

"Yeah?" My voice sounds too high. And my mind goes blank.

"I want to talk to you about something."

Here we go . . . Shit. I have to pull myself together. "Right. Listen, Jenna," I say before she can dive into whatever she means to say. "I know that you're nervous about us continuing to . . . you know, but what if we think about it differently?"

"Oh. I'm not nervous. I'm fine with it. More than fine, in fact. I just wanted to set some sex ground rules."

I'm so fucking shocked that I don't reply.

I just stand there with what I assume is my mouth open while Jenna says something about only having sex during the shoot and keeping all this from the press and being super secretive.

And then she drops the line that truly blows me away: "It's good for character development," she says, "Like method acting, right?"

Wait.

That was the argument *I* was going to make! I stare back at Jenna, half confused, and half wondering how long I have to wait to start method-acting another sex scene.

I mean, I'm not about to look a gift horse in the mouth.

"Should we maybe do some 'character work' in your trailer? Maybe right now?" I ask.

And Jenna replies with a smile.

*Thank you, universe.*

# ELEVEN

*Jenna*

I SWEAR, WE MOVE AT *Jet*-level speed to get back to my trailer. I'm ready to tear every piece of clothing off Tanner's body—to see his rippling muscles and touch my tongue to his silky skin. I also want this to last as long as humanly possible. Last night I wanted it fast—at least the first time. But now that I'm done for the day, now that I'm not second-guessing my decision, now that I know how goddamn *good* it will be . . .

I want to own him the way he owned me last night.

"I need you right now," he says as he closes the trailer door behind us, presses me against the wall, and lowers his lips to my neck. "So bad," he whispers huskily in my ear, the warmth of his breath giving me a shiver.

I step away from him, slowly, purposefully. I stay totally silent but make sure my eyes let him know that this isn't me going cold again. This is me playing what is about to be a very, very fun game.

I drag my hand from my neck down my chest, across my collarbone and then around and around my breasts.

"What are you doing?" Tanner asks. "Besides driving me completely and totally insane."

"I'm showing you where I want you to put your tongue."

Tanner lets out a tiny moan, like it is literally paining him not to be inside me right now.

I fucking love it.

"Permission to approach?" he asks.

"Granted, but I'd just like a little nibble on my right ear first."

Tanner moves over to me, then stops. He stands inches from my face and just stares at me.

"What?" I ask, suddenly self-conscious. "What is it?"

"I just want to take you all in, before you take me all in." It's cheesy, and he knows it, but it makes me smile, which was exactly his intention. How is it that Tanner still knows me so well?

But then, don't I still know how to drive him crazy, too? Maybe this is why first love never seems to fade, because it imprints so deeply. He's practically in my DNA.

Tanner cradles my face with his hands then draws me toward him and gives me that requested nibble around my ear. It's bliss. His teeth graze my skin so that it pricks with delicious pain, the perfect amount.

Now I'm fretting because I gave his tongue a whole map to travel, and I'm wondering if I can I hold out that long before getting him inside of me.

I'm still fretting as he shifts his hand to my back and pulls me into him. I sink into his body, and with that one move all my wishful thinking about this slow moving indulgence is gone. His mouth meets mine and we kiss, slowly at first. We both know how fast and fiery it can get if we don't deliberately take our time.

But that kiss grows and intensifies. Seconds later I'm totally absorbed. Our tongues are dancing in a paced and perfect rhythm. My heart starts to beat in step with every jut and dart and lick. It's bringing me to a place I haven't been in years, a depth of intimacy that I thought I'd left in the past with Tanner.

I want this kiss to last forever.

Then, Tanner pressing up against me reminds me that there is much more beyond our mouths. I feel his rock hard cock against my leg, and I remember I want that too.

I move his maddeningly soft lips from my own mouth down along my neck. Tanner responds just as I'd hoped. He licks my skin then gives me tiny sucks that send chills up and down my body. I moan, which just makes him nip and suck a little harder.

I have to have more.

I take Tanner's head and move it down to my breasts.

"Permission to nibble on these too?" Tanner asks.

Instead of saying anything, I arch myself toward him, my body telling him all he needs to know. I'm overwhelmed by his scent, his warmth, his proximity. Tanner James is a force of nature, and the hurricane of desire he's stirred up in me is a raging Category Five.

Slowly, slowly, he unbuttons the black silky shirt I'd thrown on after taking off the sports bra I was wearing in the scene we just shot. He doesn't tear it off like I expected. I watch as he leisurely undoes each and every button with the same fingers that I'm wishing were in between my legs.

I wait, semi-patiently, for him to discover what's waiting for him.

Who the hell am I kidding? The wait is killing me.

"Fuck, yes," he says as he finishes with the last button and peels the shirt off my shoulders and arms to discover that I didn't put my own bra back on in Wardrobe, instead enjoying the feel of my breasts against the soft fabric as I'd made my way over to him with exactly this moment in mind.

Now I'm standing in front of him, half-naked and exposed.

I don't need to look down to know that my nipples are pink-tipped and rock hard. They're throbbing, soaking up Tanner's gaze, desperate for his mouth. He quickly delivers, and my body lights up when his lips hit my skin. His sucks and tugs are like electric shocks straight to my pussy.

I moan over and over and over again. My knees buckle, and I can barely stand.

Tanner catches my weight and cradles my body with one arm, using the other to tickle my left tit as his mouth wraps around my right.

It's the world's hottest game of Twister except my body is the board.

I want his body to be the board too. I want to twist around him, want to coil and twine.

As if he can read my mind, Tanner releases his mouth and stares up at me. "Can I take you to bed, Jenna Stahl?"

"Yes, please."

I'm surprised I have the willpower not to scream it so loud that everyone still on set can hear. Tanner must be able to hear the excitement in my voice, because his eyes darken and he smiles before bending down to lave my nipples one last time. He's worshiping my body, and every second of it is heaven.

"I love the way you taste," he says.

"Like this?" I slip my hand down the waistband of my leggings to slide a finger through my wetness. Then I bring it to his mouth and watch his eyes roll back as he sucks my finger clean. I'm pretty sure my eyes roll back too, at the feeling of his rough tongue on my sensitive fingertip. At the carnal promises he's making.

Abruptly, as if he can't stand another second of waiting—which I understand because I can't stand another second of waiting—he turns with a growl and leads me the five paces from the middle of the trailer to the small back bedroom. It's cramped and dark, which only makes it seem sexier and more illicit. I feel like we're Rose and Jack in that vintage coach aboard the Titanic. This trailer has windows, too.

I want to see if we can steam them up just as much.

I'm pretty sure I let out a little squeal of glee as Tanner places me down on the bed. I stare up at him, his angled jaw and deep blue eyes and the sharp stubble on his chin that I can already imagine rubbing down my stomach and between my legs. He's just as hot today as he was the day that we met.

And I want him just as much.

My body agrees. I'm so wet I'm sure I won't even need his fingers to prep me for his cock—but I want them.

"Shirt. Off. Now," I command, desperate to feel his skin on mine.

Tanner quickly obeys, throwing his T-shirt over his head and revealing not only his rock hard abs but an impressive bulge peeking through the top of his famous Calvins.

He is on top of me now, his torso upright but his legs straddling my stomach. I prop myself up on one arm, leaving my other hand free to explore his perfect body. I take my hand and move it down from the tip-top of his ear, down around his neck, through the peaks of his collarbone, then across his chest muscles. I gently run the tips of my fingers across his nipples.

Now it's Tanner's turn to moan, to wordlessly tell me how much he enjoys this.

I follow the cue, replacing my fingers with my mouth on his chest, while stroking down the ridges of his stomach until I reach the very top of his pants. This time Tanner stops me.

"You first," he says, and I'm not about to protest.

He watches as I start to shimmy out of the leggings.

"I missed that stomach," he says as my hands touch there. "And those hips," he says as my pants slip down around my hipbones. "And that ass. God I missed that ass. No panties? You're such a naughty, perfect girl."

My heart trips and my eyes widen at his use of my old pet name, but I don't have time to dwell before his hands are on me, grabbing each part that he's named, giving them a squeeze before he peels my pants off the rest of the way.

"And these legs, and these knees and these ankles and these feet." He runs his mouth along every part.

I let my legs fall apart, so wet and ready for him to move up to where I want him, but instead he just stops and stares for a moment.

"And your perfect pussy. I missed that the most."

I watch the bulge in Tanner's pants get a little bit bigger. Maybe I own him already—or is it still?

My chest tightens at the thought. Tightens and bursts, like it both hurts and thrills me to have that thought.

And then I'm not thinking anymore because he slides his face up between my thighs and blows. The cool air shocks my clit and excites it all at once, and I automatically start to reach down to relieve this need he's kindled in me, but he stops me.

"This is all mine."

I trail my right hand over my left breast instead, pinching and swirling around my nipple. He watches with hungry eyes. He always loved to see me pleasure myself, and I've loved to perform since the very first time I did it for him. I moan at my own touch just to make him a little jealous. He dances his mouth around in responding torture, hovering just above my pussy where I want him.

Such a fucking tease.

I cry out in frustration, and finally, he pities me.

His face dives forward, and he strokes up me with a flattened tongue. I let out a hiss of delight. He licks me until I can't breathe, until I can't tell where he ends and I begin. I buck underneath him as my orgasm hits hard, but he doesn't stop, and I can feel a second rolling in on the heels of the first.

"I need you inside me," I say as I try to push his head away, but he fastens onto my clit and sucks, while still obeying me by slipping two fingers deep inside my body. I'd meant that I wanted his cock, but when he crooks his fingers and finds my g-spot, the shuddering spasms of an even bigger orgasm push aside any disappointment.

"You're so fucking wet," he whispers, as he continues to dive in and out of me, marveling at the way I grip his fingers inside me, at how easily he can still make me come.

"And I need my cock inside you." Finally, finally, he crawls up over me so I can undo his pants with shaking hands and run my fingers over his throbbing dick through his boxer-briefs. He's leaking at his crown, and it's obvious he's as desperate for this as I am.

I need to feel him sliding in and out, the base of him pressing against my clit with each stroke. The very thought of it has my lower belly tightening already. My breaths come fast in anticipation as he pulls his underwear off to allow my hand full access to the heavy, hard shaft bobbing above me. I squeeze him gently once, then guide him directly to my entrance and lift my hips, pressing into him as he presses into me.

As wet as I am, my orgasms have also made me tight, so it's a long, slow glide to fit him completely within me.

But once he's completely sheathed, I feel like I'm finally whole.

"Holy shit, Jenna." Tanner's voice quivers just a little, betraying the effort it's taking to hold himself still instead of giving in to the impulse to just fuck wildly. He's already throbbing as if he could come any second, and part of me wants to urge him to let go and take what he needs.

But a bigger part of me knows it's better this way. Better to take a moment and wait. Once he adjusts, once my body adjusts, he'll be able to take his sweet time, and I'll benefit from every second of his impressive erection.

God, I've missed his cock. It's not the only thing I've missed about him.

Our eyes meet, and something snaps into place between us. Something not quite fixed, but no longer as broken as it once was.

It scares me.

Tanner opens his mouth, but I'm not ready to hear what he has to say. So I cut him off with good old-fashioned body talk. I contract my inner muscles around him as I push my hips up a bit higher, letting him sink deeper inside me.

"*Fuck,*" he says, instead of whatever he was about to say. I sigh with both relief and satisfaction as the pressure hits me exactly the way I've been longing for.

I grab a pillow from the top of the bed and scoot it under the arch of my back so that my hips can rock up even higher into his shape.

And then he begins to move.

Tanner makes slow and long strokes. Every single one brings me closer and closer to total breathlessness. Each one pierces me with pleasure. I rock my hips up with a quick motion to let him know I'm ready for him to go harder, faster. He responds with the same intense thrusting at a slightly faster speed. It's too much already. I want to release it all, but I also want to savor every single second.

I grab the back of his neck with both hands to bring him closer, then I move my fingers to his hair and give it a little tug like I know he loves. I wrap my legs around him and arch up even higher than even the pillow allows. He's so deep inside me. It feels so fucking good.

I think I tell him so, but my words come out garbled as he shoves in deep, again and again.

He quickens his pace as I slide a hand in between our stomachs to play with my clit. We fall into a perfect rhythm, and I know I'm close to another orgasm. Tanner is too. I can tell by the way his forehead wrinkles. He always makes that expression when he's close to climax. I move one hand down to his ass, to feel the perfect muscles as they clench and release with each stroke, pulling him farther into me while at the same time I tighten my grip around his neck with my other hand so that I can bury my own head inside the crook of his shoulder. I bite down, hard, totally unable to control myself. He responds with a moan that says, *bite again*. The pressure is building and growing inside me so much that I'm afraid if I bite again I'll break his skin.

Instead, I let out a ragged moan. I'm close. So so close.

"Are you gonna come for me?" he asks. "Come *with* me."

All I needed was to hear him ask for me to let go, and suddenly I'm there. We explode around each other. Ripples of pure bliss gush up and down my body as Tanner releases inside me. I shudder, clenching my legs and body tight around him, dragging my climax out as long as possible. We rock together, letting every wave crash, not pulling apart even after they're over.

He lingers inside me as his breathing slows, matching my own. He leaves little kisses all over my neck, then collapses into my arms, holding me for another moment. He presses his forehead against my chest, and it occurs to me that I could stay here forever.

How did I ever let him go?

# TWELVE

*Tanner*

TWO WEEKS AFTER WE HAD sex in the trailer, I've lost count of how many illicit trysts we've had. To be fair, there may be no way of counting the infinite ways we've discovered to please each other. Or how many ways I've made her come. I have a key to her room. She has a key to mine. We're all in on this method-acting thing.

The only way I know I'm actually in Canada is from the address on the bottom of the hotel stationery that I like to scribble dirty notes on for her to find. I certainly haven't seen anyone or anything but her. The whole closed-set plan has been more of a relief than I'd figured it would be. Not only has it given Jenna and I the freedom to sneak around without anyone noticing, but it's given me a break from the papz. I hadn't realized how much a part of my life flashbulbs were until they were gone.

Comparatively, the occasional guest asking for a selfie as I cross the lobby coming or going from the set is no big deal.

I've been in Hollywood for so long, it's almost a shock to realize how normal people live.

Meanwhile, while we've fucked each other blind off-set, Jenna had the idea that we should be a little distant to each other when on set, to throw people off. She's curt but professional with me; I'm nice but not overly attentive to her. It's supposed to seem like we got off to a rocky start with that first fight scene where Jenna almost decked me in the face, and though we worked it out and are back on track, we haven't become the best of friends.

Jenna named it *Operation Trailer Trash,* in reference to our little sex den. But she can't say it without laughing, and I can't hear it without getting a semi.

All of which is to say that, for the first time since this whole crazy fling started, I'm dreading walking into Jenna's room.

She's waiting for me on the bed when I swipe my card over the electronic sensor, wearing nothing but a gorgeous pink nightie-thing that shows off her creamy breasts to absolute perfection. She kills me with how sexy she is. I have an instant hard on, and I dive for her, knocking her over in a heap of giggles and kisses.

"So I was talking to Angela—" That's all I get out before she's pushing me off and straightening her nightie.

"No."

Yeah, that's the reaction I was expecting.

"You haven't even heard what I'm going to say yet!" I protest anyway, trying to get my hands back on those perfect tits.

"It's *no* no matter what!" she says. "Why were you talking to her, anyway? I thought we agreed she's a shit-stirrer." She pouts prettily at me, folding her arms across my intended targets.

"Because no matter what we do agree on—and, yes, she's totally into drama—the studio hired her for a reason. Jenna, we've gotten a lot of leeway here with the closed set and shooting outside the States. But we have to make an occasional appearance. We both know the only reason this movie is getting the push it is, is because of *us.*"

She stares at me for a second, and then closes her eyes in resignation and lets her hands fall. Finally. I replace them with my own, and gently knead her breasts until she's pressing into me and ready to listen.

"I know you said you didn't want to go to this thing tonight. But it's just a party. And it's a surprise for Polly's birthday. If we don't go, we look like assholes, and it's even more obvious something's going on when we're the only two who don't show." Her mouth opens as if to protest, and I catch her off guard, sliding my first finger inside before she can say anything.

She sucks on it as I pull it out slowly. Goddamn, that sends shocks straight to my dick.

"I guess if it's for Polly, we have to go," she says, her eyes on my now wet finger. "I just don't know how to do this. I don't know how to be normal with yo-*oh!*" She breaks off with a squeal as the finger I've just pulled from her mouth finds another warm hole to slide into.

"I thought maybe an orgasm for you before, and then one for me after?" I make my most serious face at her, as though this is a scientific endeavor. She bites her lip to hide a smile.

"Maybe I could act normally then," she pants as I drag my finger out.

"But not now." I add another finger and push back in.

"Not now." Her hips slide lower on the bed, closer to me, as the pink silk rides up.

"We'll ignore each other all night. I won't tell anyone about how much I love eating your pussy." I grab her hips with both hands and pull her the rest of the way to my waiting mouth.

"We'll . . . *fuck* . . . flirt with other people." Her hands tangle in my hair as I fuck her with my tongue. "And I won't think about how hard you just . . . made me . . . come!" She ends with a trembling groan as I ride her climax out, suddenly more excited about the party than before, knowing that my turn awaits at the end.

She takes just long enough getting ready that my hard-on has calmed down when it's time to walk through the lobby and out to the limo the studio ordered, but when she bends over to climb into the car and I can see straight up her dress to the little black thong she's chosen, I realize I'll be fighting this battle all night.

In front of the swanky hotel hosting the party, I make a show of chivalrously helping Jenna from the limo, and we pose for a few extremely formal pictures.

"No touching," she murmurs to me, and somehow I manage to keep my hands to myself.

Once we get to the rooftop lounge and part ways, I expect everything to relax. Sure there are quite a few strangers here, but it's mostly industry people. I toss off a wave at Micah Preston, an actor I've worked and partied with, who's dancing with his girlfriend Maddie Bauer, a new up and coming director I'm dying to work with. Since they're between me and the bar, I cut in just for a minute, swinging Maddie close to tell her how impressed I was with her debut film last year, before swinging her back over to her man.

As I make my way off the floor, I catch Jenna's eyes for the barest second before she turns in one smooth move to grab a glass of champagne from a passing tray and the arm of a girl I'm pretty sure I've seen in toothpaste commercials.

Now they're the ones between me and the bar, so I give her ass the merest brush as I walk by in search of a top-shelf tequila. I've hardly even begun to examine the choices on the neon-lit glass shelves behind the bar top before I sense someone next to me. Someone who smells like orange blossoms. I start to look over but she hisses at me.

"Don't look."

I can't help but laugh. Naturally, the bartender chooses to serve her even though I was there first. I can't blame him, although the way his eyes linger on her boobs makes me want to punch him in the nuts, but I count to ten under my breath and let it slide.

I let Jenna order lemon drop shots for her and Toothpaste before asking, "Why aren't we looking at each other?"

"This place is crawling with gossips," she stage-whispers back, still staring straight ahead. "Including professional gossips. Angela invited the press team. You need to cool it, Tanner. No grab-ass."

"I like grab-ass," I tell the bartender, since I can't look at her.

"Me too, man," he says.

"Uh, cool. I'll have a Sauza 901, chilled." I slip him enough cash to cover all the drinks plus a large enough tip that he's probably thinking I want to play grab-ass with him.

"Save it for the chick on the dance floor, then," Jenna says as she slides her shots off the bar and walks off without so much as a backward glance. I know, because my head whips toward her at that remark.

Is she . . . jealous? Of Maddie Bauer?

Interesting.

I say cheers to the bartender and take my drink in the opposite direction of where Jenna just walked off. There really isn't much over here but the pool, and the night's still a bit too young for anyone to be hopping in to splash in their underthings. I fold myself onto a couch that's made for smaller people than me and cross an ankle over my knee. There's a chill to the breeze up here that's a nice contrast to the warmth burning down my throat from the tequila.

"Tanner James. I thought I saw you walk out here," comes a woman's flirtatious voice from over my shoulder. I brace, expecting Angela to be lurking behind me, but I'm pleasantly surprised to see Amber Jacobs instead.

Amber is one of the only female sound engineers I know, and a total badass. She's petite enough to fool people who don't know her into complacency, but I've seen her reduce grown men to tears on more than one set. Hollywood is a very small town, so I've had the pleasure of working with her on a number of films. It was a happy surprise to see her on the list for *Reason To Love*.

"Why's the star of the show sitting alone?" Amber asks as she makes her way over to me.

"Just taking in a view of my whole kingdom," I say, expansively indicating the empty pool with a wave of my arm.

"Your kingdom's waiting inside to yell surprise to the queen."

I half-stand to go inside and join them, but I won't be missed in there, and I'd rather chat out here where I can hear myself think than inside where the EDM beats are pumping. In that brief motion, though, I see that Jenna and Toothpaste have been joined by an older guy. I'm pretty sure he's one of the execs from Three Spots, the guys financing our movie.

*Oh, good*, I think, *she can schmooze while I enjoy myself.*

"Keep the king company?" I ask Amber.

She sits down next to me and clinks my glass with her own. I notice her drink immediately, because she must be the only woman here without either champagne or a vodka soda.

"Whiskey?" I ask, impressed.

"Bourbon. I'm a Kentucky girl, originally." She flips her red hair over one shoulder, in a gesture I've noticed often accompanies the prideful statement of a born-and-bred southerner.

"No kidding. I just got back from Louisville a couple months ago. We shot *The Bridge* there."

"Oh, right. I went up for that job but didn't get it. I was dying to shoot back near my hometown. My parents would have gotten such a kick out of it."

"Well you should have called me. I would have used my kingly powers to make them hire you."

"If only I'd had your number."

I startle. Is Amber flirting with me? When I look at her again, she gives me a huge wink and grin that tells me she's fucking with me, and that she's very aware of my reaction.

I shoot a glance in Jenna's direction. She's staring but quickly turns back toward Richard Thurgood. I notice her friend is gone, and it's just the two of them now. I narrow my eyes, but it isn't my business. We're meant to be flirting with other people, after all, and the more time she spends flattering the bigwigs, the less time I have to.

As long as flattering is all it is.

"So what do you think of the shoot so far?" I ask Amber, politely trying to keep the conversation flowing while also keeping one eye pinned on Jenna.

"Best crew I've had all year. Polly Kemper runs a tight fucking ship. Jenna Stahl is the one that's really blowing me away, though."

"Jenna?" At her name, I turn my full attention back to Amber.

"Yeah. She's good. It's a cool feeling to realize you're one of the first people to see a performance that everyone will be talking about. Like, not only is she spot on in the dramatic bits, her comedic timing is *way* better than yours. No offense. But really, who knew models could be funny?" She takes another swig of her bourbon and side-eyes me.

A chorus of *surprise!* announces Polly's arrival inside. I wait until it dies down before I answer Amber's question, even though it was most likely asked rhetorically. "I knew."

It takes a second before Amber remembers what she'd asked. I see it in her expression when it clicks. "You knew about her acting or her humor?"

"Both. I always knew she had the chops. It's exciting to see it all come together for her."

"And do you know how nice she is to the crew?" she asks, tossing her hair again.

"I know," I say simply.

"And do you know how good her ass looks in that dress tonight?"

"Oh, I fucking *know*," I moan before catching myself.

Amber laughs out loud and claps, and my hand makes a little *cut it* motion at her.

But I do grin. Amber deserves kudos for that move.

My gaze flicks back to Jenna who is no longer pretending to listen to the man in front of her. Instead she's just staring at me. Me and Amber.

She's *so* jealous.

My grin widens.

Then Thurgood snatches her attention by grabbing her chin and moving it back to him, and my grin immediately turns into a clenched jaw.

"Any idea where she got that dress? It's so cute."

It takes effort to refocus on Amber, but somehow I manage. "I'm not sure, but I'll ask her," I say with gritted teeth.

Amber wraps a curl around her finger. "You don't have to. Just tell me what it says on the tag."

And then I don't have to force the focus at all, because Amber is 100 percent insinuating I have access to Jenna's wardrobe, and not the one on set, either.

I start to panic as I down the remainder of my drink.

"Oh. Looks like I can ask her myself," Amber says.

That's when I see Jenna walking directly toward our couch. This is bad. Very, *very* bad. The second Amber turns her laser-focused interrogation on Jenna, she'll suspect that I've been telling tales outside of school.

"Hey guys," Jenna says with a smile that's pure acting. "Must be an interesting conversation, since you missed the surprise part of the surprise party."

"Very interesting," Amber says slyly. "I was just asking Tanner—"

I cut her off sharply by holding up my glass.

"And that was very rude of us. I should say hello and get a refill, care to accompany me?" It's hardly a question, since I've already firmly fastened my arm around Jenna's.

She glares down at the link between us like she's going to pull away, but then Amber speaks. "Tanner, we should definitely catch up again soon."

That's all it takes for Jenna to tighten her arm in mine and start turning us away. I don't miss the redhead's eyes on us the whole time.

"Sure. Watch the kingdom while I'm gone."

She's cackling to herself as I rush Jenna away.

"Your kingdom?" Jenna quips once we're out of Amber's earshot.

"Inside joke," I say, which is rude, because I know it will piss her off. But I'd rather have her jealous than freaking out about what people suspect or know about the two of us.

Jenna starts to walk me over to a little banquet, but I pause at the bar, holding my empty glass up toward my new friend the bartender. At least he only touched my girl with his eyes.

"Should we maybe pop down here?" she says gesturing to the seats she'd been leading me toward, and from the tone of her voice, it's more of an order than a suggestion.

"Sure . . . okay." So much for going to find Polly, but whatever's on Jenna's mind is better out than in. Her expression is cold and distant, like she's about to tell me off. At least that's progress from past conflicts where she'd usually just avoid me altogether.

Without getting a refill, I follow her to the side of the lounge. We slide into the booth despite the fact that—what feels like—a thousand people are watching. Including, as she herself told me, half of IK PR.

If Jenna is going to make a scene, this is about the worst possible spot in the whole bar.

But, though a scene is what I expect, a scene is not what I get.

"How's your night going?" she asks instead.

"Um . . . fine." I'm confused. "You?"

"Okay. It's loud here."

That's when it hits me—Jenna has no real agenda. She's not about to ream me out for flirting with Amber. She's not even questioning me about it. She's avoiding the conflict entirely. Just like Old Jenna did.

But I have no patience for that anymore.

"What are you *really* thinking right now?" I ask, leaning in so she'll feel a little bit pressured. "Why are we over here?"

I can tell Jenna's surprised that I'm being so direct. Good. Maybe it will push her to be a little more honest, too.

"Nothing! No reason," she says, trying to be nonchalant. "I just. You know. What do you, uh, think about that bartender's mustache?"

"Forgettable. Don't lie to me, Jenna. That's not why you brought me here. Are you mad at me?" I pause. "Are you *jealous?*"

"No!" she snaps, quickly. Too quickly. "I'm not jealous. I mean, I was. But then Richard Thurgood . . ."

The second his name is out of her mouth, I'm on high alert, attuned to her like a guard dog. I didn't like that hand on her chin one bit.

"What did he do?" I growl, moving closer to her, my protective instincts taking over from my conscious knowledge that I shouldn't be so close to her.

"Offered to *make me a star,*" she says mockingly. "I mean, I've heard that kind of shit before, but I guess I was just naive, thinking that once I landed this role, men would stop asking me if I wanted to fuck them for one."

The moment Jenna tells me what Richard Thurgood said, I see red. Then we both see white. A flash of light. The flash from a camera. *Fuck.*

"Cast album!" some youthful intern I've seen around set says with a way-too-perky smile. "Can I get one of you two looking a little less intense?"

"No fucking pictures!" I bark back. "Are you fucking kidding me right now?"

"Oh . . . sorry . . . I just thought, like . . . I mean you two are the whole movie . . ."

She trails off, and I feel incredibly guilty. I've officially terrified a totally harmless intern. And for what? Doing her job?

I run a hand through my hair and take a breath to cool down. "No, it's not your fault. It's just that this isn't really a good time. We'll come find you later, okay?"

"I totally get it Mr. James. I'll delete the picture right now," she says, fumbling with her camera.

"Call me Tanner. I didn't mean to flip on you. I'm just—"

But she's gone before I finish what I was saying. I'll have to smooth that over later, but for now my only concern is Jenna.

"So he propositioned you?" I ask, wanting to have a very clear picture of the reason I plan to be facing assault charges tonight. My fists are already clenching.

"He—yeah, but you know what? It doesn't matter." I can see her shutting down.

"It *does* matter. I know you don't like conflict, but this guy needs a throat-punch for saying shit like that to you." I can't just let her back down on him. I know her. It's going to weigh on her. It *should* weigh on her. I know that kind of fuckery goes on all the time in show biz but it's bullshit.

It's not going to happen on a movie I'm producing. Not with a partner I'm working with. And I'm sure as shit not going to let it happen to Jenna Stahl.

I'm half out of my seat, but Jenna tugs me back down. "Look, Tanner. Stop," she says insistently.

I pull my arm away in a huff but I stay seated.

She goes on. "If you go over there acting all alpha-male on him, it's just going to start the rumors."

I think guiltily of Amber. How many rumors did that conversation start?

"Besides. I told him I'd call his mother personally the next time I heard him speaking that way to a woman. And then I pulled out my phone and showed him her number. She gave it to me at a party in Milan a few years back."

It takes a moment to digest this but when I do, I laugh. Heartily. New Jenna for the win. Hedda Thurgood is an Old Hollywood legend known for both her fashion and for biting off more heads than Amber could ever dream of.

And speaking of.

"You were jealous, though?" It gives me such perverse satisfaction.

"Only for a second."

"Just one second?" I know she's lying. I saw how many times she looked over at the two of us on that couch.

"Aren't we supposed to be fucking right now?"

As far as subject changes go, it couldn't be more obvious, but goddamn was I glad to hear it.

# THIRTEEN

*Jenna*

KNOW WHAT BAD FORM it is to ghost a party honoring my director, and I fully expect that someone will bring this up tomorrow when we all finally roll in at the thankfully late call time. As long as Angela doesn't get anything out of it.

*Shit.* Angela.

There's no way in hell she won't be sniffing around over this.

But I couldn't stay there any longer. When my thoughts get this twisted up, I'm not fit company. Just look at me now, curled into one side of the limo, the side of my head leaning against the cool glass of the tinted window, pretending to answer emails on my phone instead of talking to the very person that probably deserves the conversation most.

I could slap myself for getting so jealous over Tanner's five-second conversation with Amber. I have no right to be jealous. We are not a couple.

I realize there's a little something else under my feelings of envy for Amber. Because while I'm sitting here staring blankly down into my little glowing screen, it's not her face I keep seeing over and over again in my mind.

It's Tanner's, yelling at that innocent intern to stop taking our picture.

That hurt.

He doesn't even want pictures of us together. I want to believe it's just about being safe with the media. That was my idea at first, too. But why was he so insistent and mean with the poor PA? He must really want to make sure there's no trace of us hitting the press even looking like we *might* be together.

It's the reminder I needed. We are not going to work—not now or ever. This party may have come at the perfect time. I should thank Amber and that snap-happy PA. Because if I'm being honest, I was starting to fall hard for Tanner all over again. And that was the one thing I promised myself I wouldn't do.

My lips curl up sardonically. What would Walter say? I don't even know if I should bother telling him how close I came to screwing up the shoot-long booty call by having Feelings. He already saw it coming.

"Good email?" Tanner asks, seeing my expression, and I glance over at him. I don't have to force my return smile, damn it. His huge grin, those friendly eyes . . . he's just charming. And now that I've had the reminder that I needed that he isn't a prince, I suppose there's no reason to stay upset. He's just obeying *my* rules, after all.

That sinking feeling can be dealt with later on. I'll buy a new pair of Manolo Blahnik's and all will be good. Probably. Maybe.

Right now, the mess in my head can only be unraveled by losing my mind completely, preferably while impaled on his massive dick.

Apparently Tanner hasn't learned the healing magic of designer shoes and hot sex because ten minutes later, he's sitting on the couch insisting that talking is the way to make things better.

"I don't believe that you're not jealous."

I roll my eyes. "Don't flatter yourself."

But he ignores my dismissive attitude. "Tell me the truth, Jenna. This isn't going to work if we lie to each other."

"*This* is not going to work because we're not in a relationship, remember? And I'm not jealous because there is nothing to be jealous over."

"Fine. Prove it." His voice is thick and his eyes dark.

And then I get it.

This is a game. He wants to think of me as jealous because it's sexy.

Something about that challenge lights a fire inside. If he wants to get dirty, that's just fine with me. I can inflate his ego and his dick at the same time.

I walk to the minibar, grab a couple bottles, and pour them into glass tumblers. Handing him one, I sit down next to him and toss my hair.

Exactly like Amber did.

"Whatcha doing?" he asks playfully.

"Showing you how very little I have to be jealous of." I hadn't smoothed down my dress before sitting, and it's riding up my thighs.

Tanner doesn't even try not to look, but I'm not ready for him to touch yet. I clink my glass to his in a parody of the toast he shared with Amber that I watched from the bar earlier.

Then I toss my hair again. "So what were you two talking about, anyway?"

"Not much," he gulps, and I wonder if there actually *is* something to be jealous of. After all, he fooled around on me once before.

Tanner's hand snakes out to grab my leg, but I stop him with a wagging finger.

"We're just having a nice conversation," I say, impertinently. "Talking about nothing much. Alone together while everyone else is inside."

"If you're being Amber in this scenario, there's nothing nice about her," Tanner says.

A thrill goes through me. Either he really isn't interested in her, or he likes a little bad in his girls these days.

I like to think I'm qualifying.

I spread my legs just a little, and he swallows again.

"Um, we talked about Kentucky a little." His eyes are glued to the tiny triangle of fabric he can see between my legs.

"Oh, Kentucky, huh? I've had their fried chicken." My voice is purposefully breathy, kittenish. "I like the breasts a lot." I run my fingers lightly over mine, bringing my nipples to stiff peaks.

"And the thighs, of course." My fingertips continue winding a sinuous course down my body, lightly brushing forward and back over the tops of my legs as I let my head fall back in appreciation of my own touch.

Tanner's breath hitches.

"Do you think it's true what they say?" I ask, drawing my hand up and under, sliding behind the elastic of my panties. "Is it finger-licking good?"

I draw my finger back out and hold it up, admiring the glistening of my own wetness. He tries to move his mouth over to find out, but I wag it again at him. I let him watch as I take a single, long lick, then run my tongue around my lips.

"Mmmm," I say. "I think it is."

While he's still entranced by my lips, I dip my finger back down to gather more, and then use it to stir his drink.

"Your ice is melting." I smile at his dropped jaw. A downward glance tells me that any thoughts of Amber that *had* been in his head are all gone now. That hard-on is all for me. As he sips his freshly stirred drink, eyes on me, I toss my hair again, to guarantee that the next time he sees another girl do it, I'll be the one he's picturing.

"Gosh," I continue in feigned distress. "That was so forward of me. Maybe you'd better teach me a lesson . . . since I wasn't very *nice.*"

I set my untouched drink on an end table and ease my way across him, my stomach pressed against his muscular thighs. He catches on quickly, with a low growl of excitement. His glass follows mine onto the table, and there's still icy condensation on his big, rough palm as he slides it up my ass, pushing my dress out of way.

He hooks a finger through the waistband of my panties and pulls them down, making a pleased sound when the little peek of my pussy under my cheeks is revealed.

I wait for a long moment as he lets the tension build before smacking my ass. Even though I was expecting it—asked for it, even—I still jump a little in his lap. He gives it a little caress before a second crack follows, this one a little harder. I can feel the blood rushing to the site of the sting, and I imagine how it must look to him, flushed pink in the shape of his hand.

Branded.

"I'm such a bad girl, Mr. James," I whimper. That earns me another couple spanks before his hand stills and his fingers delve downward where they discover just how bad I really am, drenched from the combination of spanking and excitement at playing another role I'm discovering I'm very good at.

He explores me gently with his fingers as I writhe, feeling empty and hoping if I can just wiggle back in the right way, he'll slide a couple inside. Instead, he moves away entirely, now running his hand up my side and around to the front, where he gives my nipple a hard pinch. I cry out, surprised at the way the sharp sting followed by soft pleasure echoes the sensations of the spanking.

"I think you've learned your lesson," he tells me with a wicked smile in his voice.

"Oh, I very much doubt it," I say, standing and pulling my dress off as I runway-walk back to the bedroom, knowing he'll follow without ever having to glance back. "I'm a *very* bad girl."

When he comes to his senses and gets into the room, he finds me on the bed, twirling a curl around my finger same as Amber did as I was walking toward them. But she wasn't brazen enough to be doing it naked and on her knees, with her other finger in her mouth.

"No," Tanner's voice rasps as he roughly flips and bends me so that my freshly spanked ass is in the air facing him. "You're a fucking *perfect* girl."

In a flash, he thrusts inside me, one fierce drive to punctuate his sentence. I didn't even hear him unzip his pants. I see stars as I scream out at the sudden intrusion. Tanner puts one hand on the small of my back, pinning me in place, then moves in and out of me. I jerk back and forth with the strength of his body. This must look amazingly sexy—me completely nude and getting pounded hard by this fully clothed Hollywood star.

Just imagining it makes me come. The sudden spasms around his cock earn me a gasp.

I pushed him as far as I could with my teasing, and now with my pussy clenching around him, he's lost any semblance of control. Tanner is fucking me like a man possessed, and this is exactly what I want—no, need—to drive all those other thoughts from my mind. Amber's flirtation, Richard Thurgood's proposal, the complete unfairness of Tanner's refusal to be photographed with me while still using my old nickname in the bedroom . . .

That last one sticks just a bit. The ache of it blends with the pleasure/pain of Tanner's sharp, jabbing thrusts, fading into the steady rhythm and blinding ecstasy I feel as both of our bodies tremble and quake until finally he stills and throbs inside me. I follow him off the cliff, both of us crying out our climax. The bliss rolls over and over both of our bodies until we're completely spent.

Moments later as I lie in a heap on the bed, panting, my mind remains blessedly blank, but that ache—that ache is still there. Still raw and sharp. The room is quiet except for our ragged breathing and the buzz of the air conditioner.

Finally, Tanner speaks. "So, you were totally jealous, right?"

It's a good thing he's still dressed, because it only takes a second to kick him out, leaving him completely shocked as I close the door on his handsome face for the first time since we started this affair.

Of course I was fucking jealous.

# FOURTEEN

*Tanner*

THERE'S NOTHING LONELIER THAN WAKING up in an empty bed that's usually filled with a gorgeous woman. I feel like the air's been sucked out of this room. Jenna typically fills it with her smell and her smile and the soft sound of her voice whispering in the morning. I always tell her she doesn't have to be so quiet. These hotel room walls are thick. She always jokes that she's whispering because it feels sexier in the morning, like we're keeping a secret.

Now I know just how true that feeling is for Jenna.

I guess part of me always thought she was bluffing with this whole casual sex thing. Old Jenna would never have gone that far, but this new version sent me packing at three o'clock in the morning, after some of the craziest sex I've ever had. I couldn't wait to talk about it with her— once I'd caught my breath—but she hadn't even put her robe on before escorting me to the door. That felt shitty, but not quite as shitty as it feels to wake up alone. Without her.

I childishly throw a pillow at the door. This wasn't how things were supposed to be this time. This was supposed to work. *We* were supposed to work.

And yet here I am again, wondering what she's doing while I order a fucking omelet.

I flip on the TV to try and take my mind off this pathetic morning. Some local weather person is standing in front of the giant map waving her hands at weird Canadian names. Her hair reminds me of Jenna's, and I nearly change the channel, but then she launches into all the details of the famous Celebration of Light, Vancouver's giant fireworks festival. It's today, which reminds me that we're not shooting. Fireworks and film sets don't go so well together.

But neither do free days and bored actors. Now I have nothing to do all day, and no excuse to see Jenna.

I turn the TV off and throw the remote across the room, where it luckily glances off the pillow. I have to stop pouting before I earn a rock-star hotel-trashing reputation.

But I'm not sure how to proceed, and until I have a plan, this room feels like a cage. To complete the metaphor, I start pacing like a wild animal as I try to work out what led to me waking up in my bed, alone. Jenna is pissed about *something*. I'm sure of it. She booted me for the jealousy comment, but for fuck's sake. It was funny at that point. Because, come on, we both knew she was jealous.

And it was sexy and hot and fun that she was.

It wasn't like there was any real reason she should be upset. I didn't have eyes for Amber in the first place, but now Jenna has *destroyed* any possibility of me ever looking at Amber again without picturing Jenna's bare ass over my knee and the taste of strawberries in my tequila. She knows it, too.

So jealousy can't really be the problem.

Maybe she's still worried about being seen together. I understand, I sold it to her as a private event, and then when we got there it was an industry free-for-all, with columnists everywhere.

I'm not going to look online, I know better than to ever Google my own name, but there's simply no way no one talked about us. And as close as we were sitting . . .

I'll pretend she was sick last night, and I brought her home, but how does that serve *me*? No, squelching these rumors only allows the distance between us to grow exponentially.

Then it hits like a bolt of lightning—what we need to do is *manage* them.

I race over to my phone. "Hi, it's Tanner James. Can you put me through to Angela, please? No, she's not expecting my call, but she'll speak to me."

It only takes a few minutes to arrange things, then I have the pleasure of reliving last night in the shower. If I don't jerk off in there this morning, being around her will be absolutely unbearable. Once I'm clean, shaved, tousled, and aftershaved, I select my clothes.

Like most guys, I secretly enjoy fashion a bit more than I pretend to, but also like most guys, I don't know nearly as much about it as I ought to. But I sure as hell know what Jenna likes. So I toss on some ripped jeans, not tight, but not baggy, the kind that make it very clear that I do work out—a lot. Then a button-down shirt, white with the palest gray pinstripe. After rolling the sleeves up to my elbows, I top it off with a darker gray vest.

I know I made the right choice when Jenna opens her door and visibly sweeps her eyes up and down my body—twice.

"You have a key," she grumbles, turning to walk back in, but leaving the door open for me.

"I do. But I sort of thought that was to be used at a more late-night hour. For a more late-night situation." I follow her in, watching her nostrils flare slightly as she breathes in my cologne. I wonder if she remembers that it's the same brand she brought me back from a shoot she did in Barcelona a decade ago, made in a tiny couture house that's existed for two hundred years, mostly catering to royalty before reluctantly opening their doors to the nouveau riche of Europe.

It's the only kind I've worn since.

"I'm not really up for a booty call right now, Tanner," she says.

"And I'm not here for one. Have you eaten?"

"I'm not up for a buffet, either. Thanks for the invite though."

"Look, Jenna, I just got off the phone with Angela—yes, I *know*, before you even start in. But here's the thing. We pretty clearly left together last night. So right now, everyone's making speculations about what's going on between us. The paparazzi are going to be talking about us, whether we're on a closed set or not. Now that there's a whiff of smoke, those telephoto lenses will be looking for fire."

"Shit," she mumbles, her shoulders drooping. "We made a mistake last night."

"We did *not*," I say firmly. I reach out to take her face in both hands, tilt it up to me. It's a deliberate reminder of what Richard Thurgood did, but also a reminder that I have been nothing but gentle with her—minus the spanking, of course, but she wanted that.

"You were upset. *I* was upset. We needed to leave. Leaving last night was the right decision, but now we need to decide where to lead the press. Because at this point, we're still in charge. We get to write our story. TMI can't make this what it isn't."

It's as close as I've come to telling her about the video, but if some part of me was hoping she would read between the lines, I'm disappointed. Because she doesn't.

"Okay," she says, nodding. "This makes sense. So . . . how do you propose we write our story?"

"If the gossip rags think we're hiding a secret sex thing," I raise a brow at her until she blushes, "they'll never let go. But if we go out on a very public date, tipping them off where they can find us, the whole thing will smack of a publicity stunt. And no one cares about fake relationships. Just look at what's his name—the British guy and the pop star, you know who I mean."

Jenna's starting to grin. "Everyone hated them! You're right!"

"So we just go out and do Vancouver together, me and you, all day, in public. Let them take their photos. The world will be yawning by supper, and we'll have our privacy back."

"Plus, IK PR can't say we didn't do our part in being visible. This is brilliant. You're brilliant!" She pops up on her tiptoes to kiss me reflexively. She freezes as soon as she realizes what she's doing—rewarding me with real affection for finding a way to make our non-relationship look fake. I laugh softly against her mouth to let her know I'm in on the joke, and she smiles too.

For a second we stay like that, faces together, sharing breath, happy and excited, and it feels like we really *are* Janner again.

Too soon, the moment's over, but I don't stay upset about it for long. Her delightful immodesty surfaces as she tosses her robe on the floor, revealing that she's nude beneath, and she bends over to rummage around in the pile of designer clothes strewn over the chair by the window. I don't even tempt myself by walking closer, knowing that she probably won't welcome any advances right this second.

But goddamn, do I enjoy the view.

Once she's dressed, I have the pleasure of escorting her downstairs, where we loudly ask the concierge to arrange a car service for us for the day.

People are looking, and not so covertly snapping pics on their phones. Jenna notices, and grins widely as she strikes a very awkward pose next to me, purposely leaning away from me with her upper body so that even the most casual onlooker can see her body language is reading "I don't like this."

For a quick second, I feel my insides freeze up. Does she *actually* not like this? Did I just accidentally orchestrate, not a slow burn seduction, but an "out" for her?

My worries are not entirely relieved when she playfully flashes me on her way into the Town Car, but it does take the edge off. Still, I know this little concern is going to be playing in the back of my mind all day. The trouble with letting the audience in is that now we can't be real. Or, at least, we can't know for sure what's real. I can't know what part of Jenna's character she's flaunting is for the papz and what part is just for me. Maybe none of it. Maybe all of it.

Hey, a guy can hope.

For a—what did Jenna call her? Oh, yes. For a real shit-stirrer, Angela sure threw together an extravagant day out for us on absolutely no notice. I can't imagine what she'd do for a couple that was actually willing to play her games. Although I suppose as long as she gets what she wants in the end, it may not matter.

Our first stop is Vancouver Lookout at Harper Center, and it's even more ripper than I remember from shooting *Jet*. That was back before I knew Jenna, and I remember wishing I had someone to share it with—this crazy, expansive, top-of-the-world vista. Three-hundred-sixty-degree views from forty flights up, all in a room that feels like it's enclosed in the clouds.

Angela has rented us an entire section of the observation deck, a little bubble of our own, created of glass walls. Chilled champagne is waiting for us.

Jenna is over the fucking moon.

It's one of those days where the giant cotton balls in the sky are low and fluffy so they're actually passing close to the windows of the view deck. We run around snapping selfies that make us look like we're stuck inside a big cumulus. Jenna slaps a filter on the shots that give us wings like we're angels and shoots them off into the world.

"If we want the papz on us we'll have to leave a trail," she says.

"Haven't you noticed yet?"

"What?" she asks, and I nod my head toward what she hasn't noticed in all her excitement—photographers are on the other side of the glass, snapping away, capturing every selfie and sip of bubbly.

"Angela?" Jenna asks, popping immediately back into her fake mode. She waves at them while doing another weird lean-in.

"Yeah. She's good." The light mood from a moment before is gone, but this "us against them" thing is bonding us in a different way. Jenna tells me five times how much fun she's having while we're whisked off to our next destination, one I requested specifically, knowing what a nature lover Jenna is.

The mountains have always been her favorite thing about LA, but the San Gabriels have nothing on the Canadian gem that is Grouse Mountain.

The view from the top makes the Vancouver Lookout seem like a joke. It's acres and acres of lush green pines that aren't found in southern California. The sky tram drives all the way up to the peak to give an insane view.

"Ooh, are we going to get champagne in this one, too?" she asks as we walk up to the Skyride.

"Not *in*, exactly . . ." The look on her face as we're beckoned up to the rooftop deck to ride up the mountain on the *outside* of the tram is utterly priceless. The car begins its smooth ascent, and the wind rushes through her gorgeous hair, lifting individual curls to stream out around her head.

She's perfect.

I move closer to snuggle up to her, but she's stiff, frozen in place.

The anxiety I felt earlier is suddenly back with more force than it takes to power the tram up this mountain.

"Are you okay?" I ask, my voice catching just a little. Did I misread her? Was she really faking all the fun for the paparazzi?

"I don't mind heights. And I don't mind cable cars. But being outside of a cable car, this high in the air, is surely nothing God ever intended." Her voice is small, and a few words are carried away by the wind, but her white knuckled grip on the bar and the few words I heard were enough to understand.

I'm relieved and about to gather her to me to keep her mind off her nerves, when I glance up and see a couple photographers have beat us to the top and are shooting our ascent.

Even though it makes me feel like a real asshole to leave her panicking, pics where she looks stiff and terrified with me standing a couple of paces away will show the public that all the cuddling has been for show.

The crowd of photographers gives us space when we get to the top, hanging back as though trying to snap a picture covertly. Jenna's visibly relieved when we disembark, and waiting for her, I have another surprise.

"Have you ever heard of a beavertail?" I ask, nodding toward the media in case she hasn't seen them yet.

She gives a tight nod in response and takes my hand, holding it stiffly and far from her body.

"Is that . . . an animal part or a sex thing?" she asks carefully, giving me side-eye.

"Better than the first, almost as good as the second. It's a pastry covered in different toppings."

"Wait, there's a *restaurant* in this heaven?" she says as I walk her toward the entrance. "Thank God. I'm starving." Her eyes catch mine and glint wickedly. "I burned a *lot* of calories last night."

My grin is too genuine, and I have to lower my head to hide it.

When I look up again, Jenna has selected a beavertail covered in maple—"When in Canada, eh?" and is utterly thrilled to discover, when the cashier hands her the fried pastry, that it's the size of her face.

The sun is gleaming through the windows that surround the entire place, and the halo filter from before can't touch the angelic look of pure light and joy she now wears. She runs over to a bar stool that's positioned directly in a ray then flips back to me with a giant smile.

"Take my picture!" she says, holding the giant beavertail up to her head as comparison.

"Happy to," I hear a voice reply.

It's not mine.

Jenna and I both freeze for a second. A few stools down at the bar is a guy with a long lens camera—another paparazzo. Although we knew they were around, it's the first time we've had to directly address anyone of them.

"So, is Janner back together?" he asks as he snaps a shot of Jenna, and then motions for me to join her.

I know I need to manage this moment. This was my idea, so I should take charge.

I walk over to where Jenna is sitting at the bar and smile for the camera.

"Yes!" I say heartily and over-loud. I wrap my arm around Jenna. She props an elbow on my shoulder, and I almost crack up at how over-the-top her pose is. "Now, can't you see we want privacy?" I'm stiff in my delivery, and the only thing it seems we need is a to-go box because there's no way that Jenna is eating that entire beavertail in one sitting.

The photographer snaps a few pics then shakes his head with a frown. He disappears a minute later into a dark corner to check the shots on his screen.

"Oh my God, that was amazing," Jenna laughs when he's out of earshot. "You're a pretty good actor, I suppose," she teases. "As far as co-stars go."

I *am* acting, but it's not the paparazzi I'm putting on a show for. My pretending is for Jenna. I'm trying to convince her I don't feel anything for her and that's a lie.

And, as she smiles happily and rips off another bite to hand me, I realize I don't want to pretend anymore. I don't want to play the role of boyfriend. I don't want to spin this story a minute longer.

I want to be with Jenna for real.

But before I can have any sort of future with Jenna, I have to find out what happened to our past.

# FIFTEEN

*Jenna*

WELL, IT'S TRUE WHAT THEY say. There is nothing like a fake date to make you wish you were on a real one.

Actually, no one says that, but they should, because I've learned how true it is all afternoon. For the past six hours Tanner has whisked me around town from one perfect spot to the next on our pretend date.

I have seen more gorgeous vistas on this PR excursion than I have in my entire real life. Of course the views are real. It's the relationship that's not.

How many times can I remind myself that I wanted this? That I asked for—no, *insisted* on—it?

At least as many times as I've wished things were different today, I suppose.

And it's funny, but I would have sworn Tanner has been feeling the same. I was positive he was going to pull me into his arms on the cable car, but then he held himself back.

Because I said sex only, I remind myself. I never added a "hold me when I'm scared" clause.

Then, again, on top of the mountain, there was something in his eyes. Something that didn't look a thing like acting. Something that looked an awful lot like—but it couldn't be. Probably just a trick of the light.

After all, if he was feeling things for me, he would have been kinder to the intern last night.

Perhaps New Jenna should just be brave and ask him exactly what he envisions for the future, what happens when the photogs go home. What happens when *we* go home.

But there's every chance the answer will be that we continue on our separate ways. Because that's the right answer.

So why do I keep hoping that he'd give me the wrong one?

When I compare the Tanner I've gotten to know over the past weeks with the one I fell for back then, it's almost amazing how little he's changed. He's more muscular, for sure, his hair's less shaggy and more coiffed. His confidence is now born of pride and hard work versus the swagger of youth, and the tiny crinkles around his eyes when he smiles weren't there when he was a teenager.

But besides all that, he still knows just how to make me smile, make me happy. Make me come.

So I guess the other question is, if he's still fundamentally the same person, as I believe I also am, then why did I believe things would ever end anywhere but here?

Because of course I want more from him than sex. I want all of him.

And it will always end this way, with me painting a target on my heart and handing him an arrow.

For now I'm just going to focus on enjoying the champagne and oysters that we're currently enjoying in a window-side table. Naturally, the little cluster of guys taking our picture attracted a group of curiosity-seekers, so basically we're eating in front of a full audience.

"Do you think this is what it felt like to be in an olden-time royal court?" I ask, changing the direction of my thoughts. We haven't talked about anything meaningful all day. Too many people listening.

"What do you mean?" Tanner asks, expertly detaching an oyster in mignonette from its shell.

"You know. Eating in front of the entire village while they gawked at you."

"Oh, that. Meh. You get used to it," he says, far more focused on stealing the last lemon wedge from my plate than on the retinue just outside the glass. I stare doubtingly at him until he finally looks up and meets my eyes.

"You will, too," he offers.

It hits me suddenly that after this movie comes out, no matter what the critics think of it, I'm guaranteed to be dealing with this kind of attention for as long as the buzz lasts. And despite having wanted this break forever, I wonder if I'm ready for it.

The panic must show on my face, because Tanner turns his full attention from the food to me.

"Hey. I know you inside and out, Jenna. And you've got this. There's nothing this world can throw at you that you can't handle. You're tough, you're cool, you're talented as hell, and you're a total badass. So rest assured that no matter what happens, you'll handle it with grace and style, just like you always do. Okay?"

"Yeah. Okay." I nod.

"You know, I think we've done enough. Want to head out?"

He must really not want to carry on the charade any longer.

And I can't either.

"We can't—" I start, intending to tell him that the sex is over, that this right here is the end of the affair. That in order to be the fierce woman I'm capable of becoming, I have to get him out of my bed to get him out of my head.

But he's already speaking. "Let's ditch the shutterbugs and take a walk. Just me and you. Today was so amazing, but I wasn't really present for any of it. I was so focused on making sure our story was being told the way we want that I missed all the fun I wanted to have with you."

In spite of everything, my heart lifts along with my hopes.

Then Tanner flashes me his classic smile, the one that roped me in all those years ago. It starts on the right side of his mouth then curls over to the rest of his face so that both of his perfect dimples are on full display.

And I guess I really am the same person I always was, because even knowing what I know, I realize I've already fallen in love with Tanner James all over again.

That's the only thought ringing through my head as we go through the motions of taking care of our tab and walking outside for the now-familiar awkward pose.

"What a great night, Jenna," Tanner announces in front of the crowd, with all the subtlety of a twelve-year old in a school production. "We should go back to the hotel now."

"Yes. Together," I add, my distraction only making this better.

"Well *that's* not a publicity stunt," a girl in front snickers to her friend, and I see several other people snort and agree.

"I thought they could *act* at least. Must really hate each other," someone else adds.

It's almost too easy. We don't even have to try to lose them. We walk to our car, and pull away without a single person following.

And why would they? We played them like fiddles all day.

If I'd ever doubted my acting abilities, today would have put that to bed permanently. Regardless of the relative realness or fakeness of the date, we managed to convince half of Vancouver that we could hardly stand to touch each other, when in reality the chemistry between us takes work to ignore.

After a few deceiving turns to make sure no intrepid reporter is following us, we have the driver drop us at Creekside Park. Tanner leads me down for a walk along the harbor. The almost full moon is gleaming off the rippling water, and the docked boats are bobbing on creaking ropes. Those and our footsteps are the only sounds.

We walk for a long while without speaking, the air between us growing tight and taut with the heat and flare that burns constantly when we're together. The attraction that we hid from the crowd all day is so strong now that we've unleashed it, and I find I'm suddenly shy.

I think we're on a real date now.

And I think I like it.

Eventually, words come and conversation trips and stutters as we talk about the weather and the water. He asks me if the breeze is too chilly for me enough times that I eventually realize he's just looking for an excuse to put his arm around me. Does he feel this same fumbling that I do?

Or am I reading too much into this?

I try not to think about it. Try to just live in the moment.

A mile or so later, we're holding hands freely, swinging them lightly between us. The few words have become a torrent, and, if this really is a date, it's the best date I've been on in a long time.

"I can't believe you're not going to name it *The Jet!*" I laugh, when we're deep in the middle of a game of *name your future yacht.* "Or, like, *Jet Stream.* It seems obvious."

"First of all, what kind of a douchebag do you think I am? Wait, don't answer that." He elbows me playfully when I open my mouth. "And second, boats are always women. So she needs a womanly name. Like . . ."

"The Jenna?" I do a Vanna arm, displaying my imaginary namesake.

"Meh. It's okay."

I shove him, hard enough to make him wobble a little too close to the edge of the dock. He grabs for my waist to stabilize. His touch warms my body instantly, and I hold him for a moment before our bodies separate to continue walking.

"Well I'm going to name my boat *The Squan*," I say, as our hands clasp again.

"Oh, cool. Like the town where your family has a beach house," he says.

"Wow. You remember that?"

"Of course." He stops walking for a second. "Is that where you went after?" The tone in his voice has changed, and I notice a heaviness in his eyes.

"After what?" I ask, but there's a knot in my stomach, and I already know the answer.

"After you took off." He's serious, and it makes my chest tighten.

This is not a conversation I'm prepared to have right now. Or ever. If I ever decided to move forward with him, it would mean a necessary forgetting of the past, a revisionist history in my mind and heart. It's the only way I could get over his indiscretion. Not by rehashing it.

But Tanner seems set on talking about it. "We had an apartment together. You took all your things. You were gone so fast. I had no idea where you went."

I drop my hand from his and wrap my arms around myself. "Does it matter?"

"Yes. It does." He pauses, waiting for me to say something, and when I don't he adds, "Please."

That's the word that kills me. I owe him this.

Sighing, I glance off into the distance, unable to look at him while I dredge up the past. "I moved into one of the apartments that the modeling agency keeps for the girls, until I could find my own place," I confess, softly.

"No, you didn't. I called the agency, and they had no idea."

"They lied for me." I drop my arms and turn and face him. "And you know what? You only called them once, so it wasn't exactly hard to do." Now I'm getting serious. If we're going to be telling the truth, then Tanner should remember his own.

"I should have called more times," he admits. "I took off to Australia, and I didn't try hard enough to explain the truth to you. And that's my fault. I still haven't told you, and I should have the first day of our shoot."

Those words hit me hard. They're not what I expected, but they're what I need. Still, I don't know if I'm ready to hear it. I try to brace myself, but I'm shaking and I can't look at him when I ask, "The truth about Natalia? You loved her, didn't you?"

"Oh, Jenna." His tone is so gentle that I do look up, and so the tenderness in his eyes catches me, and I can't tear my gaze away, no matter how painful his next words will likely be. No matter that my own eyes are already watery.

"The truth is that kiss wasn't real," he says. "An asshole with a film crew pretending to be a big publicist approached Natalia. He told her he was putting on a big celebrity charity kissing contest. I should have called you, of course I should have. I know that now. But at the time, I didn't think it was any bigger a deal than an acting job. I put on a performance and never expected to hear about it again, unless I got a notification that a check was being delivered to the children's hospital in my name. But there was no charity. The crew sold the footage to TMI, and I never saw you again."

And because I'm looking in his eyes, I can see that the words he speaks to me are absolute truth.

And my heart breaks all over again as I raise my trembling hand to press against my mouth.

"It wasn't real," I repeat, my voice cracking.

"It wasn't real."

It feels like a seven-ton boulder has been lifted from my chest, a weight that has pressed against me from the moment I first saw that stupid video. I can breathe deeply for the first time in years. Tanner never cheated on me.

"But then why didn't you try harder to tell me?" I'm confused. Such a silly misunderstanding could have been cleared up easily. Even if I was avoiding his calls, he could have found a way to reach me.

He lowers his eyes. "Honestly? I was afraid."

"Afraid of what? That I wouldn't believe you?"

"I was afraid you were giving up your dreams for mine." I wrinkle my brows in question, and he asks, "Why did you turn down that audition for that Judd Stow movie?"

That came out of nowhere. I shrug, not remembering right away.

"What about the Zanetti series?" he asks next.

"That conflicted with my schedule for Marisa's Closet," I say, defensively.

"You would have nailed the part for the new Supergirl if you'd gone for it," he says, confidently.

That one I *do* remember. I'd canceled that audition because I'd wanted to go to an award show that Tanner was hosting.

Wait.

My eyes sting as I start to put together where his questions must be leading. "I wasn't good enough for you. You didn't try to come after me because you were embarrassed by me. You wished I was an actress instead. That's what you're saying, isn't it?"

I try to step away, but Tanner pulls me closer. "That's not what I'm saying at all. If anything, you're too good for me."

"Then I don't get why you're bringing up all this stuff." I'm stiff in his arms, unable to look at him until he gives me a good reason.

"You canceled so many auditions, missed so many opportunities. Because of *my* career. I was afraid you were giving up all your chances of becoming a star because of *me*. I was afraid I was in the way of your dreams."

I open my mouth to disagree, but then I close it again. Is Tanner right? Did I put my acting career on hold for him?

I think back to that time, to all my fears and worries. The same fears and worries that have plagued me over the last ten years. "I might have put some things off so I could be with you," I admit, putting my palms against his chest. "And you thought if you pushed me away, I'd focus more on my dreams? You sacrificed *us* . . . for *me*?"

He nods. "I didn't want you to give up all your chances and then one day find you resented me. I wanted you to stop putting me before you. I loved you too much for that. So when the video happened and you left . . . it killed me to let you go, but I did."

A tear slips down my face. I'm a mess inside with conflicting emotions from his latest confession. On the one hand, he's so dumb. The idea that I'd be better at *anything* without him is ludicrous.

On the other hand, it's the most incredible thing anyone's ever done for me. And I wasn't worthy of it. Because I've been lying to him and to myself about those early days.

"I can't believe you did that for me, Tanner," I tell him, my hand cupping his cheek. "I know you meant well. But the truth is that I was using you as an excuse. I was scared too. Modeling came so naturally. I barely had to work for it. But acting was harder. The auditions I did go to ended in so many no's. What if I never got any further than that? What if I failed? I couldn't bear to face that."

His eyes soften, soaking up my painful confession. "Oh, baby, you could never fail. Not if you get back up again after you're knocked down, and you always get back up. And look where you are now! You're so strong and self-assured and about ready to break out in your first major role. A whole New Jenna."

I blink back another tear. "There is no New Jenna, Tanner. Everything you see right now? It's only been because of you. I started faking my confidence to get me through seeing you again. And I've only been able to keep it going because you make me feel strong."

He studies me. "I don't believe that. You've always been this strong."

"How can you say that? I run away from everything. I ran away from the best thing in my life because I was afraid. It's all an act." Tanner's shaking his head even before I finish my sentence.

"It's not an act. This is *you*. I've seen this you on the catwalks of Paris and on the covers of magazines. You just haven't let yourself believe that you were meant to be a star anywhere other than the modeling world, when I've known all along that you shine everywhere."

I know he believes what he's saying. And it's true that I've always been pretty brave, all models are to do what we do.

But I know the truth.

I am only the woman I want to be when I'm with the man standing in front of me.

# SIXTEEN

*Tanner*

'VE IMAGINED THIS MOMENT FOR years, what it would feel like to clear the air. How she would react. I thought for so long I only wanted the vindication of proving that I didn't cheat on her. That I would never have cheated on her.

But here when it's actually happening, while we're laying everything out on the table, the thing I want most is for her to know how sorry I am. And that she still owns my heart.

I pull back so she's forced to look up. "Jenna, I have never stopped loving you. I have never stopped wanting you in my arms. And I've been a fool for waiting this long to say that."

The tears spill over, and down her face.

Worried, I use my thumbs to brush them away.

"It's fine. They're happy tears," she says. "I thought you stopped caring about me a very long time ago. But today . . . I really hoped you hadn't."

I'm so relieved.

Despite the chemistry between us—the constant pull, the amazing sex—her messaging has been consistent from day one that we were keeping it casual. I had no reason to believe she'd want to hear any of this from me.

I have one card left to prove how far I'm willing to go for her, and it's time to lay it on the table. No more secrets between us.

"I have something else to confess," I say.

She stares at me, concern written on her face.

"I tried to move on over the years. I dated other people. But I never stopped thinking about you. Finally, I realized I never would. So, uh . . . well, I'm sort of the one who put the Janner movie together. It was my idea."

The world stops. There's total silence. Even the water seems to stop its bubble and babble for a moment.

Jenna doesn't move. She doesn't say a word. She just stares at me in complete and utter shock.

And then, after the longest three seconds of my life, her lips shift into a giant beaming smile, and she leaps into my arms.

"That's either the most romantic thing on earth, or the most self-indulgent," she says between kisses. "But I'm awfully glad you did. And, see? I told you I needed you."

And just like every time we kiss, it seems, it becomes apparent that we aren't going to stop with kisses. I call our driver to come collect us, and we make out like teenagers while we wait. As we hop in the car, I fire off a text to the concierge to fill my room with rose petals and candles. I don't just play a romantic in the movies.

And the happy surprise on her face when she sees it is enough to make me understand why men do it so often on screen. *Such a simple gesture for such a sweet reward*, I think, as she pulls me in for a long, deep, slow kiss.

We've kissed a lot lately, and a lot before, but each kiss since I've realized I still need her in my life has felt different.

We aren't kissing the people we thought we knew anymore. We've finally shed our characters—not the ones from *Reason To Love*, but the ones we've been playing for the world. Each tentative touch of our tongues sends a shiver down my spine, this private conversation of ours that's totally unscripted is the best love story ever told.

We explore each other for what feels like ages, just inside the doorway, by the glow of candlelight as the smell of roses mingles with orange blossom in my nose. Barcelona's couture perfumerie may work for another two hundred years, but nothing can ever capture this scent, with its undercurrents of hope and arousal. Finally, I pull back to gaze at her dilated eyes and kiss-swollen lips, my eyes moving down and up at this out-of-my-league woman I've somehow gotten lucky with, not once, but twice over.

And then I realize—she's worn red.

I think she realizes at the same time, because her sensuous mouth widens into a devilish smile as she steps out of her dress, letting it pool at her feet, and stands before me as proud and nervous as she did the first time we made love.

I'm not wearing a tie tonight, but I take off my vest and toss it onto the couch, a signal that I understand.

This is our first time. For the second time.

I hold out my hand, and she silently accepts. Together, we walk into the bedroom, my perfect girl and me.

"You ruined me for anyone else, you know," she whispers.

I don't answer. There's no need to. I didn't say that to her all those years ago to brag, and I don't need to gloat now. It was never about being a sex god—though, I won't shun the title. It was about *us*, as much then as it is now, and the connection that only two people in love can possibly have. And maybe since she was my first real love—and I was her first love—it makes our connection deeper. I was the first man to have been inside her, the first man to both love her and make love to her—how could we not be forever marked by that?

And even though the sex that first night was movie-perfect, the real standard we set that night was how much we felt for each other. I'd gladly trade in every kinky, sexy fuck we've had this shoot to make sure she knows I still feel that much for her tonight.

She steps ahead of me to recline on the bed and removes her bra. This time, there's no breathless concern that she'll know what to do and how to please me. She teases me with a smile and toys with her nipple while she waits for me to join her.

My shirt cannot possibly come off fast enough.

"You know if you rip it, you can afford another one," she says.

So fuck it. I do. I need to be on top of her right this second. On top of her and inside her, and thanks to the destroyed shirt, I almost am. I start low, at the arch of her foot, adoring every inch of her skin with my mouth. My tongue hums along her landscape as I move slowly up her leg. I run along the smooth surface of her thighs and feel her skin prick with goosebumps at my touch.

Jesus, I love how I affect her. How I can make her shiver and moan and writhe. How I can make her use my name like it's a curse and then like it's a prayer. It does more for my ego than any award or public recognition could.

As I move to nibble along the inside of Jenna's thigh, she brings her hands up to run her fingers through my hair. The feel of them on my neck and ears and scalp makes my dick throb, and it's tempting to rush to bury myself inside her, to relieve the ache.

But I'm not going to hurry this. I have a lot of lost time to make up for.

I make my way to her pussy, sucking and licking along the length of her folds, avoiding the place she wants me most, until she's soaked and squirming. Then I nudge my tongue under her hood and lave her clit with long, lush strokes.

She comes quickly, her fingers twisting in my hair as she moans out a string of curse words begging me to stop.

But I don't stop. Instead, I clamp down on her bud, sucking the tender swollen flesh that brings another orgasm crashing through right on top of the last.

Fuck, she's so gorgeous. So sexy. So perfect, twisting under my mouth from pleasure. So entirely mine.

My balls are aching and my cock is heavy like lead when I finally strip the rest of my clothes and climb over her. I want to love all of her, want to cherish her breasts and her flat stomach, but I also can't wait any longer to be inside her. So I settle for attending to her body with my hands, gently plumping her tits while I center myself between her thighs. As though it's where they belong, she hooks her legs up around my waist, and I slide into her wet, tight warmth.

We sigh in unison when I'm seated perfectly to the hilt. And then we rock together, our foreheads pressed to each other, both of us murmuring words of love and desire. I move in and out of her unhurriedly, letting the next round of pleasure twine inside of her in slow, languid furls, and when she finally crests again, I speed my thrusts up until I'm climaxing with her, diving off the edge, hurling into a sea of ecstasy.

We're sweat drenched and exhausted when I roll off her, but I take her with me, wrapping her tight in my arms. "I love you, my perfect girl," I whisper, kissing her temple.

"Tell me one more time," she says, sleepily, her eyes already closed.

I do. And then I tell her again.

I'll tell her a thousand times. I'll tell her every day until we die, because now that I have Jenna back, I'm never letting her go again.

# SEVENTEEN

*Jenna*

O PENING MY EYES THE NEXT morning gives me the same feeling as a child on Christmas morning—there's something wonderful waiting for me, and nothing in the world can dampen my enthusiasm about it.

I peek over at Tanner in the bed next to me. He's still asleep, so I slip out of the covers and go splash some water on my face. It isn't until I glance in the mirror that I realize I've been grinning the entire time.

Out in the living area, I grab a room service menu. Strong tea is on my mind. But then a stray memory creeps in, this silly thing we used to do back in the day when we were a new couple and couldn't fathom being far enough from the bed to go to the buffet.

I actually giggle out loud. We were so ridiculous. I decide to surprise him with a re-creation. The guy I place our order with doesn't quite fail to mask his concern when I tell him we only need two sets of silverware and mugs to go along with the Belgian waffles, lox, avocado scramble, corned beef hash, breakfast burrito, and one each of every side on the menu.

What can I say? We have the kind of sex that works up an appetite.

The knock on the door comes just as Tanner is ambling out in nothing but Calvin Kleins, and as the room service attendant ushers the massive amount of food in, I can't quite decide which looks more delicious—him or it.

"Did you order one of everything on the menu?" he asks.

"Pretty much." I pour a large mug of coffee for him and doctor it up the way he used to like it, with cream and no sugar.

"Any western omelets in there?" He hands me my tea, fixed the way I like to drink it—sugar, no milk.

"No . . ." I say, suddenly worried that I should have just asked him what he wanted before going on this ordering binge.

"Thank God," he says. "I am sick to death of eating those without you."

I'm not entirely sure what he's talking about, but who cares, because he's just dragged a piece of waffle through some whipped cream, and he's holding it out for me to eat.

I lick every single bit of the whipped cream off the fork, then dab a little on him so I can lick that, too.

It's not long before this escalates. Twenty minutes later, we're forced to call down for more whipped cream, and I've just performed the tastiest blowjob of my life.

The food isn't any less delicious now for being cold. I've spent so much of my time off set sneaking around with Tanner that I've forgotten to work in a good room-service experience during our Vancouver filming, and that used to be my favorite part of fucking in hotels.

Well, we're more than making up for that today.

We take our time enjoying the dishes, making a mess of crumbs in the bed during the process. Finally, we've slowed down on our bacon intake. I take my plate back out to the living room, then return to the bed to crawl beneath the covers. Tanner meets me there, and we lie on our backs, my head on his shoulder.

Neither of us has addressed the fact that shooting will end tomorrow.

"So," I say. I'm not avoiding this discussion. I'm really not. I'm just easing into it.

"So?" He lifts the hand of the arm I'm lying on and trails his fingers up and down my waist.

"What's next, Tanner?" I roll over so I can look at him, but he continues to stare at the ceiling above us.

"Los Angeles. Warm weather. Press junkets. Premieres." He's listing our commitments to the film, not to each other. "I start filming the next Jet movie in another month. You have a zillion offers to sift through." I roll my eyes at his exaggeration about my newly blossoming acting career. "Rinse. Repeat."

"Yeah." Even though he's talking about our jobs and not us, it's kind of the same thing. These are all things we'll have to navigate as a couple. We might have thrown the press off our scent for now, but it's only going to take one sighting of us in our sunglasses and sweats grabbing an early-morning bagel for TMI to realize they've been played. And then there we are, back in the limelight, prey for the next desperate guy with a camera who wants to make a buck off of spreading rumors about us.

It's been heaven having all this private time with Tanner, but it's not realistic to think it will last. How will we weather the addition of the rest of the world into our relationship? We certainly didn't fare well last time the outside got involved.

"Maybe we should just take things day by day," Tanner says, finally glancing toward me and meeting my eyes.

"Yeah. Okay." I roll onto my back again. My stomach knots.

I understand the challenges we face—the public, our past. Last time we were a couple there was a ton of attention on us. Now, it will be ten times worse. And I haven't exactly had a chance to prove that I wouldn't make the same exact mistakes when the articles casting doubt on us inevitably appear. It does seem like what we have is precious enough to deserve some protection. Precious enough to take our time.

Except . . . is it dumb that I don't want to waste any more time?

We've already spent a decade apart, why wait any longer to be together?

I sigh, loudly enough for him to squeeze me tighter. Then I close my eyes and nestle into Tanner's embrace. I'm not going to waste this time together freaking out about the challenges we face. That's almost all I've done so far, when instead I could be enjoying the feel of his long, hard body against mine. I can pretend the outside world doesn't exist for just a tiny bit longer.

After tomorrow, our real life begins.

———— ✦ ————

OUR REAL LIFE STARTS WITH a bang. Or more accurately, a camera flash.

The news from Vancouver has filtered down to La La Land, so I've hardly set foot in the terminal before there's someone in my face asking me if it's true that Tanner and I have been faking a relationship for publicity.

I don't know what to say.

We flew separately hoping to avoid a scene like this, but we probably should have had a plan for this situation, just in case. "Take it one day at a time" didn't cover what our official line would be. I have several voice messages that came through the minute the plane landed from Carrie, asking the same thing, and I can't even bring myself to call her back.

As much as I'd love to just say, *we're together but we're keeping it private for now*, even handing it off to our teams to handle feels like a violation. We need to have a real talk about this, Tanner and I. Tonight.

And in the meantime?

"No comment," I tell the reporter as I get into the car that's waiting for me. I take it to my house to drop off my baggage before continuing over to Tanner's. My fingers fly across the keyboard of my phone as I desperately try to catch up on all the emails I've ignored over the past couple of weeks.

Carrie texts me, *How come you can give me opinions on scripts within a half hour of receiving them, but not tell me what's up with you and TJ?*

I ignore it.

Walter texts seven times a day, so I ignore him too.

Finally, finally, we pull up to a gated community, where the guard checks my ID—and my boobs—before waving us on. When we pull up in front of Tanner's house, I'm floored. The massive Spanish-style home is a far cry from the bungalow we'd shared together back in the day. It serves to remind me yet again, that he is in a very different world than he was ten years ago.

Do I fit in this world of his? Is that why he wanted to take it day by day, because he's not sure yet?

He greets me at the door, shirtless and smiling, and my worries melt away. How can I feel insecure when this tall, gorgeous man is waiting for me?

Inside, I drop my bag and embrace him. "Your house is insane," I tell him. I know, intellectually, that he's worth millions, but seeing it in person is still amazing. The kid I knew back then on the brink of seeing all his dreams come true has now realized every single one of them.

"Let me show you around," he says, picking up the bag and slinging it over his shoulder. "After all, you're going to be spending an awful lot of time here."

"Let's go straight to my favorite room first," he says, grabbing my hand and leading me to an ornate set of double doors at the end of a hallway across from the living area. When he flings them open, I squeal.

"Your own theater!" Everyone has their own idea of what success means to them. When we would lay in bed and sort through Tanner's post-*Jet* scripts, chatting about the things we wanted—wanted to do, and wanted to be—he always said he was going to have a home theater. It would have a full bar, a concession stand stocked with his favorite things—smoked almonds and rice crackers, hummus and baba ghanoush. He'd host viewing parties for all his friends, so that the ones doing Lifetime movies could see themselves on a big screen, the ones shopping their student films around could show them to his new friends with small production companies, and everyone could enjoy the pleasure of throwing spoons at The Room any time they wanted.

I spin around, taking it all in. There are red velvet curtains, chairs, and loveseats, the bar in the back, and a full-sized refrigerator that I assume is probably more convenient than an actual concession stand if you don't want to walk back and forth from the kitchen a bunch of times.

Overwhelmed, I kiss him until we fall onto a loveseat.

"Did you get yours?" he asks when my head falls to the side so I can kiss down his neck. I know what he's talking about. When Tanner met me, I had all the free things I could ask for. The hottest looks before they even touched the runway, invitations to premieres and restaurants and boutiques. There's no better way to get buzz than to have beautiful people linked to your brand. I had an apartment I liked just fine that I almost never saw because of my crazy travel schedule.

No, I had all the physical things I could ever have dreamed of. My barometer of success was a secret, something I never even told Tanner.

All I wanted was more of a concept: *home*.

I had the furniture, I had the art, but I never had the feeling. I thought I was getting it when I moved in with Tanner, but it only took a few months for me to lose it.

Now it's starting to feel like it's within my reach again, but I'm still not ready to share.

"Almost," I whisper in his ear, gazing at the goosebumps I raise on his arms as I do. I suck his earlobe into my mouth, loving the way he responds.

"Is this the first room we're going to have sex in, then?" he asks.

"The first?"

"We have to christen my house," he says, plucking the straps of my tank from my shoulders so he can shimmy my shirt down to enjoy my bra. It's red, and matches his theater, which makes him smile.

"Oh, yeah?" I unbutton his shirt as he slides a thumb under my bra cup to pinch my nipple.

"And then we'll have to christen yours, of course." He pulls my breast out to suck where he was just touching, and I arch toward him.

"Of course," I say. I give up on his buttons and relax back, letting him feast on me.

A phone rings. We ignore it. It rings again, followed by his cell.

"I'm sorry." He pulls back, but groans when we break contact.

"No, I get it." And I do. We wouldn't have a theater to christen if he wasn't popular. He answers the phone and mouths "my agent" at me, walking out of the room to talk. I pull my bra back up and take in the theater again. It really is amazing.

And when I'm with him, I really do feel like *home* may not be a place after all, but a feeling.

"Good news and bad news," Tanner says, walking back in. "Good news, we get a week in New York where no one cares what celebrities are up to. Bad news, we have to leave right now."

"Oh, Tanner!" I can't believe the shitty timing. "I can't go to New York, I literally just booked a guest role on *Karma Kills*. Like on the way over here. And it shoots all week. What are you doing, do you have to go?"

"It's Saturday Night Live," he says.

Well, yeah, he has to go.

And fuck. I wish I could go with him.

"You were hilarious last time," I tell him, not too proud to admit that I watched his episode multiple times. "Who's the musical guest?"

"Nick Ryder." I throw myself back in the loveseat and make a dramatic pose.

"He's my favorite! This is so unfair. How will we christen the house now?"

"Do it without me." I know the look on his face right now, and it's dirty. "Finish the tour while I'm gone, and christen them solo. Send me pictures, playing with your pussy in every room." I'm wet already, and the idea of teasing him for a week alleviates just a little of the anxiety I feel about how this relationship will work if we're forced to be apart so soon.

"Okay," I say.

"That's my perfect girl," he says, dropping a kiss on my head and getting back on the phone to make travel arrangements. I pull out my phone, too, and text Walter. Having Tanner gone just as soon as we've landed is convenient for my bestie, for sure. It's been way too long since I've seen his face, and I owe him a long conversation. I text:

*In-person catch up Saturday, SNL slumber party at my place?*

He doesn't even bother to respond with words, just a string of booze emojis. Looks like I'll survive the week after all. But there's still something I haven't done, something I need to do now. So as Tanner walks out the door, I call after him.

"I love you."

# EIGHTEEN

*Tanner*

NEW YORK CITY IS GRUELING any day of the week, but it's totally brutal when you're prepping to host *Saturday Night Live*. The minute I touch down at JFK, I'm getting e-mails and calls from the writers about sketches and jokes and whether or not I can sing or dance or tap dance. The host of SNL gets in deep with the writers and cast. I'll be sitting in on pitch sessions and have to be available to test out ideas. I might even get to write a skit if I want. It's exhausting.

It's also one of the most fucking amazing things I've ever gotten to do. And I've gotten to do it twice now. I'm a lucky man.

It would be more amazing if Jenna could be here with me, but this life is a lot of watching each other do cool shit from afar.

By day two I have been hunkered down inside the offices at Thirty Rock for what feels like a month, but it's just Wednesday, late afternoon. Things are going well so far. We've got a solid cold open down and enough sketches to take into the first pitch session to the executive producers tomorrow. That means I may actually get out of the building before ten tonight. Not that I know what I'll do with myself once I'm free. Every hour I spend away from Jenna makes me realize how much I want to be with her every second of the day. I'm making a total fool of myself with these writers because all my suggestions for skits involve Janner, and I spend all my free time on my phone with her. I'm probably coming off like a real lovesick dickhead.

Well, that's because I *am* a real lovesick dickhead.

We break for dinner way earlier than usual, which means six pm instead of eight-thirty. I head into the cafeteria to make a plate and see if anyone is talking about an evening plan. The writers will probably hang to work but there will be cast or crew members that will probably invite me out for a drink. I should go just so I don't end up back at my hotel watching crap TV.

Still, I'm not really in the mood for going out. I miss my girlfriend, and that makes me shitty company. Besides, if I just head to my room, maybe we can Skype, or watch the same movie while we chat on the phone.

I run into Kevin, the line producer, en route to the sushi station. They don't skimp at SNL, which is always nice. "Hey, man," he says, "Any interest in a beer? Some of us are hitting the club."

I consider it for a moment, wondering if I ought to just go and stop mooning around. "Nah, thanks, though. I'm going to get back to the hotel early tonight so I can make sure I talk to my girlfriend before I hit the sack."

"Girlfriends," Kevin says. "They're good with those short leashes."

I smile and shrug, but I'm not complaining about my leash.

Then he asks, "So you and Jenna Stahl are officially back together?"

He has to ask because I haven't specified that fact. I now realize that I've talked about Janner, but I haven't said anything about Jenna and I being a couple again. And I really *shouldn't*, not without talking to her, seeing as I was the one who said we should take it slowly as far as the public goes.

I'm so caught off guard that I respond by bumbling, "Well, I don't . . . we just . . . ten years ago we were . . . you know . . . everyone knows, but now. I don't know. We're figuring it out."

"Oh. Okay. Cool," Kevin replies with a very confused look on his face. And then he slips away.

I don't blame the guy.

I instantly realize how dumb I look and sound, and more importantly feel. Why the fuck have I been keeping things so *wait and see* with Jenna when I know how I feel? We've said we loved each other. I loved her for years before we arrived on that film set together. And *now* I'm going to play games? This is exactly the kind of bullshit that ruined my relationship with Jenna the first time around, and I don't want to do that shit anymore. I don't want to wait and see.

I want to put a ring on it.

*Holy shit. I want to marry Jenna!*

The minute I allow myself to think that massive thought, another idea pops into my head. I look down at my watch. It's just after seven. I do a quick Google search to find out if I can make it where I now know I need to go ASAP.

*Yep. Still open.*

And then I walk right up to the director and say, "I need to run an errand. I'll be back." I don't wait for a reply. I'm playing that diva actor card I hate, but it's totally worth it.

Fifteen minutes later I'm standing in front of the diamond engagement rings display at Tiffany & Co. on Fifth Avenue. It's the flagship store, the one from *Breakfast at Tiffany's*, one of Jenna's favorite movies of all time. For our first Halloween together she went as Holly Golightly in her sexy white button down shirt and eye mask get-up, and I was Paul Varjak in a vintage suit Jenna snagged for me at a costume shop. That night Jenna had said, with a wink, *"If I ever get engaged I want it to be with a diamond from Tiffany's. The real one."*

She probably never thought it would take ten years, but better late than never. Especially if you have the chance to get it just right.

"Tell me what you're looking for, sir," the shop girl says to me. She's young, maybe twenty-five, and has the kind of trendy style that makes me think she's up on her magazine reading. And that makes me think she knows Jenna Stahl.

And probably me.

"Hi," I say, deciding to just lay it all out there. "I'm Tanner James."

"I know," she says with a smile. "It's an honor to have you in, Mr. James."

I'm relieved that she's a professional and not fangirling the way some people do when they meet me. "Tanner, please."

"What are you shopping for today?"

"An engagement ring," I say, and her face lights up.

"For Jenna?" she whispers.

*Damn.* I'm suddenly worried about the paparazzi. About this salesgirl letting word slip about what I'm doing. Just my luck, TMI would blow my proposal before I got a chance to pop the question.

The girl in front of me seems to sense my concern. "Don't worry, Mr. James. Uh, Tanner. I would never tell anyone about anything you purchase or who it's for. Not only would I lose my job, but I also wouldn't want to ruin the surprise."

"Thank you." I have a feeling she's telling the truth, but I'm not going to throw all my faith in the stranger—I've been burned before. I realize it doesn't matter, though. Jenna knows not to believe anything TMI says anymore. It will still be a surprise.

So although I don't say Jenna's name, I don't correct the salesgirl. "Do you think you could help me find something just right for her?" I ask.

"Oh, I know I can." Immediately, she starts opening cases and pulling out rings.

It only takes us twenty minutes to find the perfect option. The third ring Jessica, the shop girl, tries on is a vintage-inspired stunner called *The Audrey.*

"Boom," I say. "That's the one." The perfect ring for my perfect girl.

"Yep," she replies. "That's the one. I just showed it to you third and not first because people are weird about buying the first thing they see. I guess it just takes some people a little longer to decide on things."

"Story of my life," I say.

The look on her face tells me she knows exactly what I mean.

I start to walk back to Thirty Rock with a little Tiffany blue bag in my hands and what I'm sure is a dumb-in-love look on my face. Two blocks in I realize I should probably hide the bag, as well as my smile, in case any paparazzi are lingering on Fifth Avenue. I definitely want to surprise Jenna, and the longer I take to propose, the harder it will be to keep it secret. Besides, I don't think I can sit on this for very long. I want to do it soon after I'm back in LA. And I want to get back to LA as fast as humanly possible.

The next morning, I call my agent's office and have them change my flight from Monday to first thing Sunday morning. There's a six a.m. flight out of JFK that will get me into LAX at nine a.m. Jenna lives fifteen minutes from the airport, which means I can get to her before she's even out of her pajamas.

If I'm lucky and she's having a lazy morning, I can just slip right into bed next to her for some wake-up sex. I'm dying for it after a week away from her, and I know she's got to be too.

With a ring purchased and a decision made about our future, I'm more anxious to get done with this trip than ever. The next few days seem to move like molasses, but finally, it's Saturday night. I text Jenna before we go live, and she shoots back a sweet *good luck* message along with some dirty talk that boosts my ego and helps me feel confident when the cameras start to roll. I'm sure it's partly because of her that the show goes off without a hitch.

After we wrap, Jenna texts me another message telling me how good the show was. I want to talk to her, but I don't want to let on that I'm coming home early. Plus there's the after party to go to. I send her a quick text back, telling her I love her, then I head over to the club.

The cast stays out until three in the morning, and I grab my luggage from the hotel and go straight to the airport after that. I'm going to be tired when I get home, but I'm going to be with Jenna, and if I have to spend all day in bed, well, so be it. Though, with her in bed with me, I'm not sure how much sleep I'll be catching up on.

She's all I think about as I sit on the five and a half hour flight back home. About touching her, being inside her. And then about more serious things, like our future together and about popping the question. The diamond in my pocket feels bulky and I can't stop patting my hand over my jacket to make sure it's still there—no way was I leaving it in my luggage, out of my sight. The longer I wear it, though, the more I long to see *her* wearing it.

*I should just do it now. Why would I wait, anyway? To make it more special? What's more special than a total surprise?*

By the time I land, I've made up my mind. It's happening today, the minute I walk in the door.

I work on my proposal speech in the cab over to her house. I change it a million times because there are so many things I want to say to her. Too many things. I decide I'll tell her that this is coming ten years too late, but that I'm glad we've had all the time to become better people for each other, me especially. I consider stopping to get some flowers, but I'm dying to get there before Jenna even steps foot out of bed so I abandon that and tell the cab to drive like hell. I'm holding the ring box in my hand for the whole car ride.

I'm ready.

I step out of the cab and take a deep breath. It's nine-thirty am. This is it. I've never felt so sure of anything.

Jenna gave me a key when we got back to LA from Vancouver, so I let myself in as quietly as possible. She'll hear me if she's already up, so my plan is to just pivot to a proposal out on the patio. But I don't hear a sound as I enter; she's still asleep.

*Perfect.*

I carefully put my bags down in the foyer and take another deep breath. For a second I wonder if this is the right decision. Not because I don't want to propose, but because I want it to be the right proposal. Will Jenna be mad that I'm doing it without talking about it first? I said we were taking it a day at a time. Should I warn her first? Hint around? Should it be more special?

Maybe I should call her and tell her I'm coming in early, then meet her for dinner at Joe's in Venice tonight. That might be a more romantic location. Is this the way our engagement story should go?

My gut says yes.

All the best parts of our relationship have been driven by instinct. The moment we first met, the night we first slept together, and the entire way we got back together this time. Our story is driven by impulse, which makes this proposal the perfect way to cap it off.

That means it's show time.

I tiptoe through the living room and into the hallway. Still no sound. I slip the ring box into my pocket and head into the bedroom. She must be sleeping. I decide I'll crawl into bed beside her and slip the ring on her finger while she's still out. Jenna sleeps like the dead, so I'm sure I can do it without her waking up. Then I'll see how long it takes for her to notice the diamond on her hand.

God, I'm so excited, it's going to be hard not to wake her up myself.

Mostly, I just can't wait to see my sweet girl's sleeping face when I push the door open.

But that's not what greets me on the other side.

The first thing I see is a man's face. A total stranger. He's sound asleep on my side of the bed. Shirtless. His arm draped across the body in the bed next to him.

I'm thrown.

Then I'm spinning.

Then I'm speechless.

And then, I'm seeing red.

"Who the fuck is this?" I yell.

He wakes up startled, as does Jenna, who I now see is the body next to him, dressed in the same blue nighty set she used to woo me into her hotel bed so many times in Vancouver.

If it's possible for physical steam to come out of a man's ears like in the cartoons, then someone ought to see if that's happening to me right now. I want to shred this place apart. I want to punch a hole right through a wall. I want to kick this guy's ass and ask questions later. Deal with details later.

Like the detail of my fucking broken heart.

"I'm Walter," the guy says, sitting up, his eyes blinking with sleep.

I'd almost forgotten that I'd asked, but that name immediately hits my ears. I know it. I've heard it before.

I've heard it from Jenna's own mouth, I realize.

*Walter? Who is Walter?*

Then it hits me—Walter is the name of the guy that Jenna claimed was *not* her boyfriend. The name of the guy she was talking to on the phone when I was outside her trailer that day. The name of the guy she said *I love you* to.

So then what the fuck is *Walter* doing in her bed right now?

I might regret what I'll do if I find out that answer. So I don't stay to find out. Instead I turn around, walk back down the hallway, through the living room and directly out the front door.

# NINETEEN

*Jenna*

'M STILL HALF ASLEEP AND so confused. Was I just dreaming that Tanner was here? I sit in bed staring at the door where I swear he was just standing. I rub my eyes.

No. I'm awake. He was here. I check the clock on the dresser. It reads nine-forty AM.

*Wait.* Tanner is supposed to come home around nine-thirty *Monday.* Is the clock wrong? Did I somehow sleep through an entire day? I know Walter and I polished off a bottle of champagne last night, but could I have possibly lost a full 24 hours?

I'm fully awake now. And now I distinctly remember Tanner yelling at Walter.

"What the hell just happened?" I ask, throwing the covers off.

"I believe your boyfriend tried to surprise you by coming home early. And it worked." Walter smiles guiltily. "I guess I surprised him, too. By being in bed with his girlfriend. Whoopsie daisy!"

I laugh out loud. Literally. It's a bursting cackle. Walter is so obviously not straight. Plus I told Tanner I was hanging with my bestie to watch him on live TV.

"Why would he freak out?" I ask Walter. "It doesn't make sense."

I jump out of bed and peek into the hallway. There's no one there. The house is silent. Did he leave?

"Well in his defense, we *are* dressed like the sex scene in a daytime soap opera," Walter says, stretching.

I look down at my negligee and back over at Walter's bare chest.

*Shit.* He's right. This doesn't look good, if you don't know my boy bestie would rather die than touch a woman's parts for any reason other than draping a new gown.

"But I swear I told Tanner that you weren't my boyfriend when he asked me during the shoot." Didn't I? I try to recall how the conversation went.

"Uh-huh, but did you tell him that I was your *gay* best friend?"

I'll be honest, I can't remember those precise words coming out of my mouth. I don't normally use Walter's sexual preference as an identifying quality when talking about him. I should have probably told Tanner, though. And I might have . . . The whole shoot is now a blur of mixed messages and steamy trailer sessions.

"Okay. This is just a little misunderstanding," I say, but my stomach is starting to knot. We're too newly back together to have misunderstandings so soon. I have to fix this. "Lemme call Tanner and explain. Put some clothes on. Just because his first sighting of you was in your undies, doesn't mean the official introduction should go the same way."

"Valid," Walter says. "But I really hadn't planned my outfit for this."

Walter grabs his trusty silk and starts to rummage through his store of clothes in my closet while I grab my cell to call Tanner. My chest is tight with guilt. He rushed home to surprise me—and what a romantic surprise—and he must have been so horrified to find me in bed with another man. And don't I know how that feels?

I dial.

No answer.

Which is fine. I try not to panic. Maybe his phone is dead. Maybe he's driving and can't pick up. Though he didn't have a car at the airport. Did he go home first and get one? If he just cabbed over, how did he even leave? Did he Uber?

I text and wait.

The message says *delivered,* so his phone isn't dead.

But Tanner still doesn't respond.

I call again. Nothing. I call a third time. Same deal.

And then it hits me. He's not picking up on purpose.

He's not going to pick up. He is giving me the total blow-off.

And now I'm pissed.

Five minutes later Walter emerges with beauty products but still in the kimono, apparently unable to find an appropriate meet-the-boy-friend outfit.

"He won't take my calls! Can you believe this? I mean, it's the simplest mistake. It's not even a mistake. It's a *misunderstanding.* No one did anything wrong. I will say one sentence to Tanner, and he'll totally understand what's going on here."

"Uh-huh," Walter says, nodding as he massages oil into his bald head.

"But now I'm not just pissed about that." I'm still pacing, my arms flying expressively as I talk. "This means Tanner doesn't trust me! He thinks I would actually cheat on him while he's in New York working. Literally everything we've been building together all these weeks means nothing to him if he thinks that I would be so disloyal, which means we're right back where we started, and Tanner James is going to break my heart. *Again.*"

"Did it occur to you that you might deserve this?" Walter says, calmly. Patronizingly. "And could you please stop pacing, you're giving me motion sickness."

"My fault? Are you kidding me?"

"Don't give me that angry face," he starts, "just hear me out. Ten years ago Tanner made what you now know was a 'simple mistake,' and you walked away without letting him explain, true or false?"

"True," I say, as my heart starts to beat a little slower and my stomach sinks a little further.

"And you were so angry because you thought he'd betrayed your trust, true or false?"

"You know the answer."

"And he called and called and called, but you wouldn't pick up, true or . . . ?"

I cut him off. "Thank you. I got the point."

"And now you know that Tanner's number one feeling after that whole charade was *how could Jenna not trust me enough to know I wouldn't hurt her like that?* True or false?"

"This is different!" I insist, stomping. "We were young and stupid back then. And we were afraid. And we didn't communicate. We're adults now. We talk."

"Which is why he knew exactly who I was when he saw you in bed with me."

It takes me a second to respond because I don't want to give Walter the benefit of being right, yet again. Finally I cave. "You might have a point."

"Age doesn't matter. Hurt is hurt," Walter says.

"Have you ever considered being a therapist?"

"Absolutely not. Other people's problems make me insane. Yours included."

"Hey!"

"Bottom line. You have every right to be frustrated, but so does he. So now you're getting a taste of your own medicine. What are you going to do about it?"

"I don't know. Keep calling?"

"Don't look at me," Walter says. "I don't know what you're supposed to do. This is your drama. Now I'm going to go shave so I can get out of here and figure out what I'm wearing once you've fixed it."

Walter heads back into the bathroom. I throw on a robe and slump down on the bed. It is time for some robo-calling.

I dial Tanner over and over and over again. I text at least ten times, too.

*Please come back. This is silly.*

*I can explain but I want to do it in person so you'll really believe me.*

*Please, Tanner. Let's not ruin this all over again.*

He doesn't respond. Karma's a real bitch, I think to myself.

But I know better this time, and so does he. He's just upset, but I will not—I repeat, not—let him get away.

"What are you going to do, honey?" Walter asks.

I know exactly what I have to do—reverse history. Maybe I ran away from Tanner last time, but he also didn't try hard enough to win me back. He knows that now, and I'm not going to repeat the same mistake *he* made, at the very least. It is Grand Gesture time for this girl, even if that means ignoring the twisting and turning of my stomach . . . and mustering the courage to do a little 'face talking.'

"I'm going to get my man back." I take a deep breath and head for the bedroom door.

"Go get 'em girl! I'm proud of you," Walter calls after me "But maybe take off your robe and put on some real clothes?"

"Uh. Yep. Good point." I turn around and rush to the closet, grab the first item of red clothing I can find—a slip dress—and throw it on for a little added color confidence. Tanner always says red is my color. Here's hoping it gives me the boost I need right now.

"Wish me luck," I tell Walter, as I throw my hair in a bun, grab my bag and open the front door.

# TWENTY

*Tanner*

PACE BACK AND FORTH on the front lawn, trying to wrap my head around what the fuck just happened.

Jenna was in bed. With another man.

Fuck.

Fuck!

I'm too worked up to stay in one place. I don't have a car, and I need space to think. I take off around the block to sort my head.

I've barely made it down a few houses when my phone buzzes with a call.

It's her.

I can't answer. I'm too mad. Too hurt. We just got back together and she already cheated on me! I silence the call.

She texts a minute later asking me to come back and talk.

Yeah, like how she came back and talked to me after she thought I cheated? Fuck that. She can sit with this until I get my thoughts straight.

I silence my phone altogether and shove it in my pocket. I'm an asshole for ignoring her, and an even bigger asshole for justifying my actions because she did it to me in the past, but my chest is aching, and I can barely breathe.

I love her. I was going to ask her to marry me!

Is this my fault for refusing to tell her I wanted to be with her for real? Because I said I wanted to take it day by day?

I could kick myself for that now. I was such a fucking idiot.

Or . . . oh God. There's another possibility, and it's the worst one of all. Did she make me fall for her all over again so that she could have the pleasure of breaking *my* heart this time?

I don't doubt Jenna's acting skills. She *is* good. But I don't think I could possibly have misread all the signs of her body, the reactions she couldn't have controlled. The way her pulse quickens each and every time I touch her. Or the way her body seeks mine out, even in sleep. The way she comes for me like fireworks.

Besides, now that she knows the truth about what happened with Natalia and the infamous kiss, it wouldn't make sense for her to follow through on any kind of nefarious plan for revenge. Especially after we opened up and realized that we both had fears holding us back.

So, what was this then? A drunken night with an ex? A booty call because she needed to come, and I didn't Skype her? Was she with that guy the whole time we were getting back together? Am *I* the asshole who's the other guy?

I don't like any of these options, but it's worse not knowing the answer. I don't know how Jenna spent all these years without resolution. I can't even handle twenty minutes.

And instead of waiting for the universe to give me an opportunity to work things out with her like I did before, this time I'm going after her right from the beginning.

I practically run the last leg of the block back to her house. I'm prepared that Jenna won't want to talk to me. She'll send him—Walter—to talk me down. She'll be avoiding the confrontation.

Just thinking about it makes me want to punch him in the nuts.

Of course I'm not going to punch him. Or anyone. I'm going to be cool, and stay there until Jenna sees me. Then I'm going to make her talk things out. Like a grown-up. Like we should have done last time.

I head up to the front door, but just as I go to put my key in the lock, it swings inward.

And standing where I expect to see Walter, is Jenna.

"You're still here?" she asks, her brows furrowed, her eyes hopeful.

Like there was anywhere else I would be when this isn't settled. Well, except for the trip around the block.

"I'm not you, Jenna," I spit. Is she planning to leave before we discuss this?

Not gonna work. I'll be here when she gets back. I'll wait for as long as it takes. "We need to talk."

"Hold on, Tanner. I need to tell—"

"No." I cut her off. "You don't get to talk. *I* get to talk. I just found you in bed with another man; that means *I* get the speaking stick now." I pace in front of her in tight strides, a caged tiger.

"Last time, *you* got the speaking stick," I continue. "You wouldn't know that, because you ran away. I see how you felt now, but what I don't see is how you were able to leave." I stop and direct my stare at her. "I was serious when I told you I love you. I thought you felt the same."

I can feel the storm of rage within me swirling. How dare she. How *dare* she?

"This is my fault for not defining our relationship. Let me give you a definition right now. The second you went to bed with me, you lost your right to fuck other guys. In case you're wondering, I wouldn't touch another woman with a ten-foot pole. And I'm just so . . ."

I trail off, not knowing the words to tell her exactly how furious and overwhelmingly *sad* I am to know that all along, she maybe just wasn't capable of loving me the way I loved her.

*Love* her.

I still fucking love her, God help me.

There's nothing to punch on the porch, but I want to destroy something. Anything.

Maybe everything. I'd burn everything beneath the Hollywood sign to the ground if it meant this feeling inside would go away.

Behind Jenna, I see that guy, *Walter*, and he's grinning. It's a real bastard move, and I think I actually growl at him.

"Hi!" he says with a little wave. "It's nice to meet you!"

With that he disappears back into the house, leaving Jenna smirking and watching me. I'm horrified that she's just going to let him stay while we talk this out, but maybe she doesn't trust me not to punch him on his way out.

"It's taken us a full decade to finally learn to trust each other again. I never thought we'd actually get back together on this movie, and I know you didn't either. But we did. And I thought that meant we were meant to be together for real. I don't know if it's because of chemistry or personality or the fucking alignment of the stars, but you and I are a perfect fit. I'm willing to do whatever it takes to make this work because I know I'll never find someone like you. I love you, Jenna, with all my heart and all my soul. Why would you want to ruin that?"

I'm out of breath, out of words. My eyes sting, hot and dry.

"Do I get the speaking stick yet?" she asks.

As much as I want to hear her explanation, I'm also afraid of what she'll say. I don't really want to hear her tell me she just doesn't love me that much. I'm broken now, but that would shatter me. I'm still hoping against hope that this is all a bad dream.

But she's staring at me, and I've learned, if nothing else, that I have to stop letting fear interfere with my relationship with her.

"Fine," I reply.

"Good. Why don't you come inside so we don't attract any attention from any neighbors . . . or TMI reporters."

Something about Jenna's tone is throwing me off. I can't figure out why she's so completely calm, but she makes a good point about reporters.

I let her lead me through the door. I guess she *does* trust me not to hurt the guy I found in her bed. Although the only possible way for me to inflict the same pain on him that he has on me would be to rip his heart out, and I'm not sure even my *Jet* alter-ego could justify that.

She sits me down at the kitchen island, in the same room with Walter. We're actually going to discuss this in front of him?

I look back and forth from Walter to Jenna, warily. But she's important to me, so I let this ride out. For now.

"Firstly," she says, "I understand how you feel. And thank you for staying and telling me. But here is the part you don't know—Walter came over last night so we could hang out, watch your *amazing* performance on *SNL*, and chat about *our boyfriends*. And then we fell asleep."

My heart starts racing all over again. "Okay, right, after 'chatting' about your boyf . . . wait. Boyfriends? As in, both of you have boyfriends?"

I whip my head around to look at Walter again. He is cheerfully making cappuccinos on Jenna's espresso machine. There are three mugs in front of him, and two of them are pink, as is the elaborate kimono he's donned.

He looks over, catches my eye and gives me an exaggerated wink.

Oh.

*Oh.*

"I . . ." The storm of emotion drains from my body, leaving me tired, embarrassed, and stuttering. Not to mention *relieved*. "But you have to admit that was really confusing . . ."

"Yes. It was. You're right. And I would have told you what to expect if I'd been expecting *you* this morning."

I can feel my ears turning pink. "I wanted to surprise you, and it backfired just a tad."

"Just a tad," Walter says, setting down fresh coffee in front of me and a tea in front of Jenna. "But let me tell you, as someone who's hated you since I met her, I'm pretty jazzed to see how *passionate* you are about her now." The arched brow and little shimmy he gives leaves me no doubt that Jenna has described our *passion* in great detail to him.

"Can we start over?" I ask.

"Nope."

And my heart falls into my stomach.

"Because you were right about a lot of things you said when you thought Walter and I had sex. And we need to address that. We probably should have done it a week ago."

With that, Walter tastefully melts into the living room with his coffee.

"Most importantly, I'm sorry. I've owed you this apology for a very long time, and this seems like the right time for it. I'm sorry for running away from you ten years ago. It was wrong and shortsighted and stubborn. When I thought you were gone, it was really scary to wonder if you'd ever come back. It's easy to assume, and really hard to swallow your pride and actually talk to someone."

She's tearing up, and holds up a finger to save her place while she heads to the bathroom to blow her nose. I get up and frantically gesture to Walter, and have to just hope he understands me because she isn't gone long.

When she's back in the room, Jenna opens her mouth to continue, but I cut her off. "Can I have the speaking stick back?"

"Sure. We don't have a stick, though."

"How about I use your hand, then?"

I reach down and take her hand in my own. Her smooth skin gives me an instant sense of calm. This morning might have started on a really sour note, but in a strange way it's actually been a great thing to happen. We've both proven beyond a shadow of a doubt that although we still fit as well as we did ten years ago, we've also grown up in all the ways that count.

The next time we are tested—and in Hollywood, we *will* be—I know we'll come to each other first.

So there's nothing that feels more appropriate now than to finish exactly what I started last night before the show.

"I'm sorry about today, too," I tell her, rubbing my thumb along the back of her hand. "I should have handled it better. But I'm mostly sorry that I didn't make it clear how important you were to me ten years ago. Instead of letting you go so that you could make your dreams come true without me in the way, I should have found a way to make your dreams come true *with* me. I wasted a lot of time not having you in my life. And I don't want to make that mistake again."

She's tearing up again, and this time I make no effort at all to hide the fact that my eyes are also shining.

"You have made me happier over the past three months than I have been in the ten years since we've been apart. I was an idiot for suggesting we take it slow. I don't want to spend another day without you in my life." I use my free hand to reach into my pocket, whip out the Tiffany ring box and fall to one knee. "Jenna Stahl, I love you, and I will always love you. Will you please marry me?"

She's in my arms before that final word comes out of my mouth.

"Yes, yes, yes!" she sobs over and over again, laughing at the same time.

I hold her tight, closing my eyes in silent thanks.

When I open them again, I see Walter had understood exactly what I was asking. He holds up his phone, where he's captured the entire proposal, and then bursts into sobs louder than Jenna's and joins us for a hug. I pat him awkwardly. I'm excited to get to know Jenna's best friend, but normally I only like one person in lingerie crying on me at a time.

"I'm going to design you the most beautiful wedding dress the world has ever seen," Walter sniffles as Jenna shifts from crying to staring at her brand new ring. "And then I'll design myself the most beautiful man of honor suit Roger has ever seen."

I stare at him, confused, and his eyes fly open wide.

"Oh! You might want to be alone for a few moments before we start the fittings . . ." he says, and I nod gratefully.

"It is absolutely perfect," Jenna tells me, too absorbed in her new jewelry to even notice Walter close the front door behind him. "Is it . . . ?

"It is. The Audrey. The perfect ring for my perfect girl," I say, then, once again, I pull her into my arms, and we start living the rest of time together.

# EPILOGUE

*Jenna*

"**A**RE YOU READY?"

We're sitting in the back of the Escalade, seconds away from walking down the red carpet for the premiere of *Reason To Love*. Tanner is beside me in his crisp, black W. Harris tux. He's never looked hotter. And from the look on his face every time his eyes land on me, Walter must have outdone himself on me, too.

I'm wearing red.

"Is anyone ever truly ready for this?" I ask, looking out at the pandemonium that awaits. After tonight, my movie is officially out in the world.

*Our* movie.

I nervously touch the chignon that Walter instructed my stylist to do as an homage to Audrey.

My career is not quite at Hepburn level yet, but I have received three movie offers since *Reason To Love* finished filming. There's a psychological thriller I'm really excited about, and a girl's-trip movie that should be a lot of fun. But my favorite upcoming project is another romantic comedy co-starring none other than Tanner James.

Apparently critics love us on the big screen together.

I can't say I blame them. We're my favorite couple, too.

But there are still butterflies in my stomach tonight. This is my first real premiere, the first red carpet I'm walking for *my* film, not just on Tanner's arm, like the old days. I take a deep breath, and glance down at my ring, a tangible symbol of the love that we share. With this on my finger, and him at my side, I'm ready for anything the world can throw at me.

We step out of the car and the screams of the fans packed outside the ropes reach a fever pitch. The butterflies in my stomach are doing back flips. Tanner can tell. He reaches over and grabs my hand.

"I won't leave your side," he promises. And I know he means it.

Outside the car, fans are screaming both our names. *Jenna! Tanner! We love Janner!* It's overwhelming and amazing at the same time. For so long that celebrity pet name *Janner* made me cringe, but now it represents where we are today, not where we were back then.

Out of the corner of my eye I catch Angela standing next to the publicist from the film. She gives a mincing little wave, and I give a giant one back. It's easy to bitch about the way she tried to manipulate Tanner and I, but in the end, getting together was the right thing to do, and not just for the box office receipts.

Up ahead we see Polly finishing up an interview with the team at *Film Week* magazine. I hear them ask her some questions about the script, the set, the cinematography. It would be lovely if that was the kind of thing we get asked too, but I know better. No one wants to discuss role prep or comedic timing with Hollywood's newest It couple.

"Tanner? Jenna? Are we ready for interview number one?" I hear a young girl in a headset ask.

"You bet," Tanner replies.

"Perfect," she says. "We'll start with the team from TMI."

My stomach sinks. The irony would be hysterical if it wasn't so terrifying. Of course the very first interview Tanner and I are forced to do on the movie that brought us back together is with the outlet that tore us apart. I wish I could think of this as sweet justice—we survived despite their best efforts—but I'm too nervous.

Tanner squeezes my hand, sensing my unease.

"Don't worry," he says, "I'll do the talking."

We both step up into the section reserved for the TMI reporter, a perky blonde wearing a teeny, tiny cocktail dress and six-inch heels.

"Hey you two," she says, "I'm Tina and I cannot *wait* to ask you a few questions."

"Jenna. I'll start with you," Tina says, "What is it like to be back with the man who broke your heart a decade ago?"

It's an intense question, on purpose. I can see the excitement in Tina's eyes as my body freezes. She knows she's got me, which was exactly her intention. But New Jenna isn't about to let this intimidate her.

I stare her down until she blinks nervously and moves on.

"How did he propose? And when's the big day? Everyone wants to know."

I keep staring silently, and Tina from TMI is starting to look like she would rather be anywhere else.

Finally, Tanner steps in. "Everything you get from us will be on the screen tonight. The rest of our story belongs to us."

God, I love him.

We step off the TMI platform and back into the red carpet fray. The rest is a total blur. We're asked a million questions about our wedding plans, but Tanner's response is all they'll get from us. Our story is ours.

And then, finally, we find our way to our seats. There's a little box of popcorn with our faces on it waiting at our seat, a cute touch from the sweet marketing department. Carrie is sitting a few rows behind me, snapping pictures of the popcorn containers, no doubt for me to share on social media tomorrow. Polly is on the other side of Tanner, looking stunning and giving us a thumbs up. I'm sitting dead center, directly next to my co-star and fiancé.

I see a flicker of light flash on the velvet fabric of the seatback in front of me. It's the light from the chandeliers catching on my engagement ring. I look down at it and smile, like I do every time I think about what the future holds for me and the love of my life.

There's the secret vineyard wedding we have planned for next month, and the month-long honeymoon to Bali that will follow. My mind wanders to what will happen once we're back in Los Angeles, as husband and wife. Maybe we'll move to Malibu like we've been talking about, where Tanner can surf every morning and I can find a new Hot Pilates class. Maybe we'll adopt a puppy and name him something that will remind us of those amazing months on set in Vancouver. Maybe we'll start trying for a baby.

Our future is a blank book, just waiting for us to fill it with love and adventure.

The lights dim in the theater. The crowd cheers. Camera lights flash as the paparazzi try to steal one more shot of Tanner and me taking in this incredible moment.

Suddenly I understand why everyone is so fascinated with my life— *our* life.

It's perfect.

HE KNOWS HOW TO USE HIS NIGHT STICK.

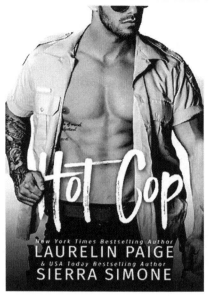

You have the right to remain sexy.

Anything you say can and will be used to get you in my bed.

You have the right to use my body to give yourself a delirious, life-changing orgasm.

If you have trouble . . . don't worry, I'm a bit of an expert in that department.

There's nothing 'thin' about my blue line, if you catch my drift, and trust me, I know how to put those handcuffs to good use.

Livia Ward wants a baby before she's thirty. And even though Officer Chase Kelly is exactly the kind of cocky jerk this librarian has sworn off, he is undeniably hot. Both of them think they can give each other what they want—a few nights of fun for Officer Kelly, a no-strings baby for Livia—but this hot cop is about to learn that sex, babies, and love don't always play by the rules.

EVEN PORN STARS FALL IN LOVE.

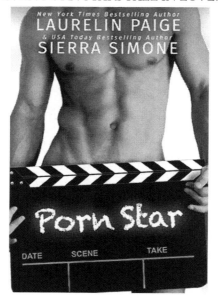

You know me.

Come on, you know you do.

Maybe you pretend you don't. Maybe you clear your browser history religiously. Maybe you pretend to be aghast whenever someone even mentions the word porn in your presence.

But the truth is that you do know me.

Everybody knows Logan O'Toole, world famous porn star. Except then Devi Dare pops into my world, and pretty soon

I'm doing things that aren't like me—like texting her with flirty banter and creating an entire web porn series just so I can get to star in her bed. Again. And again.

With Devi, my entire universe shifts, and the more time I spend with her, the more I realize that Logan O'Toole isn't the guy I thought he was.

So maybe I'm not the guy you thought I was either.

IT'S DIRTY. IT'S FILTHY. AND IT'S FREE!

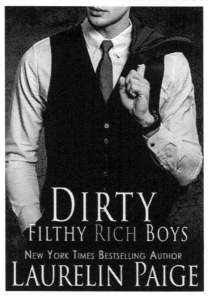

When I met Donovan Kincaid, I knew he was rich. I didn't know he was filthy. Truth be told, I was only trying to get his best friend to notice me. I knew poor scholarship girls like me didn't stand a chance against guys like Weston King and Donovan Kincaid, but I was in love with his world, their world, of parties and sex and power. I knew what I wanted—I knew who I wanted—until one night, their world tried to bite me back and Donovan saved me. He saved me, and then Weston finally noticed me, and I finally learned what it was to be in their world. Because when dirty, filthy, rich boys play, they play for keeps.

From NYT Bestselling author Laurelin Paige, discover a whole new world filled with sex, love, power, romance and Dirty, Filthy Rich Men.

Dirty Filthy Rich Boys is FREE everywhere for a limited time!

# ALSO BY
# LAURELIN PAIGE

THE DIRTY UNIVERSE

*Dirty Filthy Rich Men* (Dirty Duet #1)

*Dirty Filthy Rich Love* (Dirty Duet #2)

*Dirty Filthy Fix* (a spinoff novella)

*Dirty Sexy Player* (Dirty Games Duet #1, July 2018)

*Dirty Sexy Games* (Dirty Games Duet #2, November 2018)

THE FIXED UNIVERSE

*Fixed on You* (Fixed #1)

*Found in You* (Fixed #2)

*Forever with You* (Fixed #3)

*Hudson* (Fixed #4)

*Fixed Forever* (Fixed #5)

*Free Me* (Found Duet #1)

*Find Me* (Found Duet #2)

*Chandler* (a spinoff novel)

*Falling Under You* (a spinoff novella)

FIRST AND LAST

*First Touch*

*Last Kiss*

HOLLYWOOD HEAT

*Sex Symbol*

*Star Struck*

*One More Time*

Written with Kayti McGee
under the name LAURELIN MCGEE
*Hot Alphas*
*Miss Match*
*Love Struck*

Written with SIERRA SIMONE
*Porn Star*
*Hot Cop*

# ABOUT LAURELIN PAIGE

WITH OVER 1 MILLION BOOKS sold, Laurelin Paige is the *NY Times*, *Wall Street Journal*, and *USA Today* Bestselling Author of the Fixed Trilogy. She's a sucker for a good romance and gets giddy anytime there's kissing, much to the embarrassment of her three daughters. Her husband doesn't seem to complain, however. When she isn't reading or writing sexy stories, she's probably singing, watching *Game of Thrones* and *the Walking Dead*, or dreaming of Michael Fassbender. She's also a proud member of Mensa International though she doesn't do anything with the organization except use it as material for her bio.

*www.laurelinpaige.com*
*laurelinpaigeauthor@gmail.com*

Made in the USA
Lexington, KY
30 July 2019